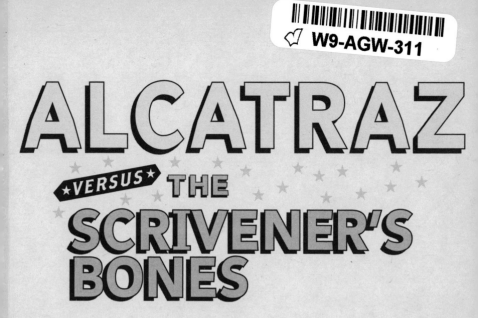

ALCATRAZ

VERSUS THE

SCRIVENER'S BONES

ALCATRAZ

VERSUS THE

SCRIVENER'S BONES

BY BRANDON SANDERSON

Scholastic Inc.

New York Toronto London Auckland
Sydney Mexico City New Delhi Hong Kong

This book was originally published in hardcover by Scholastic Press in 2008.

ISBN-13: 978-0-439-92554-9
ISBN-10: 0-439-92554-1

12 11 10 9 8 7 6 5 4 3 2 1   9 10 11 12 13 14/0

Printed in the U.S.A.   40

First Scholastic paperback printing, October 2009

Book design by Alison Klapthor

For Lauren, who somehow manages to be both the baby of
the family and the most responsible one of us all

AUTHOR'S FOREWORD

I AM A LIAR.

I REALIZE THAT YOU MAY NOT BELIEVE THIS. IN FACT, I HOPE THAT YOU DON'T. NOT ONLY WOULD THAT MAKE THE STATEMENT PARTICULARLY IRONIC, BUT IT MEANS YOU HAVE VERY FAR TO FALL.

YOU SEE, I KNOW THAT YOU FREE KINGDOMERS HAVE HEARD STORIES ABOUT ME. PERHAPS YOU'VE SEEN A DOCUMENTARY OR TWO ABOUT MY LIFE THROUGH A SILIMATIC SCREEN. I CAN UNDERSTAND WHY YOU MIGHT NOT BELIEVE THAT I'M A LIAR. YOU PROBABLY THINK THAT I'M JUST BEING HUMBLE.

YOU THINK YOU KNOW ME. YOU'VE LISTENED TO THE STORYTELLERS. YOU'VE TALKED WITH YOUR FRIENDS ABOUT MY EXPLOITS. YOU'VE READ HISTORY BOOKS AND HEARD THE CRIERS TELL OF MY HEROIC DEEDS. THE TROUBLE IS, THE ONLY PEOPLE WHO ARE BIGGER LIARS THAN MYSELF ARE THE PEOPLE WHO LIKE TO TALK ABOUT ME.

YOU DON'T KNOW ME. YOU DON'T UNDERSTAND ME. AND YOU CERTAINLY SHOULDN'T BELIEVE WHAT YOU READ ABOUT ME. EXCEPT — OF COURSE — WHAT YOU READ IN THIS BOOK, FOR IT WILL CONTAIN THE TRUTH.

NOW, LET ME SPEAK TO THE HUSHLANDERS. THAT MEANS THOSE OF YOU WHO LIVE IN PLACES LIKE CANADA, EUROPE, OR THE AMERICAS. DO NOT BE FOOLED BECAUSE THIS BOOK LOOKS LIKE A WORK OF FANTASY! LIKE THE PREVIOUS VOLUME, WE ARE PUBLISHING THIS BOOK AS FICTION IN THE HUSHLANDS TO HIDE IT FROM THE LIBRARIANS.

THIS IS NOT FICTION. IN THE FREE KINGDOMS — LANDS LIKE MOKIA AND NALHALLA — IT WILL BE PUBLISHED OPENLY AS AN AUTOBIOGRAPHY. FOR THAT IS WHAT IT IS. MY OWN STORY TOLD — FOR

THE FIRST TIME — TO PROVE WHAT REALLY HAPPENED.

For once, I intend to cut through the falsehoods. For once, I intend to see the truth in print. My name is Alcatraz Smedry, and I welcome you to the second volume of my life story.

May you find it enlightening.

ALCATRAZ

VERSUS THE

SCRIVENER'S BONES

CHAPTER 1

So, there I was, slumped in my chair, waiting in a drab airport terminal, munching absently on a bag of stale potato chips.

Not the beginning you expected, is it? You likely thought that I would start this book with something exciting. A scene involving evil Librarians, perhaps — something with altars, Alivened, or at least some machine guns.

I'm sorry to disappoint you. It won't be the first time I do that. However, it's for your own good. You see, I have decided to reform. My last book was terribly unfair — I started it with an intense, threatening scene of action. Then I cut away from it and left the reader hanging, wondering, and frustrated.

I promise to no longer be deceptive like that in my writing. I won't use cliff-hangers or other tricks to keep

1

you reading. I will be calm, respectful, and completely straightforward.

Oh, by the way. Did I mention that while waiting in that airport I was probably in the most danger I'd ever been in my entire life?

I ate another stale potato chip.

If you'd passed by me sitting there, you would have thought that I looked like an average American boy. I was thirteen years old, and I had dark brown hair. I wore loose jeans, a green jacket, and white sneakers. I'd started to grow a bit taller during the last few months, but I was well within the average for my age.

In fact, the only abnormal thing about me were the blue glasses I was wearing. Not truly sunglasses, they looked like an old man's reading glasses, only with a baby-blue tint.

(I still consider this aspect of my life to be terribly unfair. For some reason, the more powerful a pair of Oculatory Lenses is, the less cool they tend to look. I'm developing a theory about it — the Law of Disproportional Lameness.)

I munched on another chip. *Come on . . .* , I thought. *Where are you?*

My grandfather, as usual, was late. Now, he couldn't *completely* be blamed for it. Leavenworth Smedry, after all, is a Smedry. (The last name's a dead giveaway.) Like all Smedries, he has a magic Talent. His is the ability to magically arrive late to appointments.

While most people would have considered this to be a large inconvenience, it's the Smedry way to use our Talents for our benefit. Grandpa Smedry, for instance, tends to arrive late to things like bullet wounds and disasters. His Talent had saved his life on numerous occasions.

Unfortunately, he also tends to be late the rest of the time too. I think he uses his Talent as an excuse even when it isn't to blame; I've tried to challenge him on this several times, but always failed. He'd just arrive late to the scolding, and so the sound would never reach him. (Besides, in Grandpa Smedry's opinion, a scolding *is* a disaster.)

I hunched down a little bit more in the chair, trying to look inconspicuous. The problem was, anyone who knew what to look for could see I was wearing Oculatory Lenses. In this case, my baby-blue spectacles were Courier's Lenses, a common type of Lens that lets two Oculators communicate over a short distance. My grandfather and I had put them to good use during the last few months, running and hiding from Librarian agents.

Few people in the Hushlands understand the power of Oculatory Lenses. Most of those who walked through the airport were completely unaware of things like Oculators, silimatic technology, and the sect of evil Librarians who secretly ruled the world.

Yes. You read that right. Evil Librarians control the world. They keep everyone in ignorance, teaching them falsehoods in place of history, geography, and politics. It's kind of a joke to them. Why else do you think the Librarians named themselves what they did?

Librarians. LIE-brarians.

Sounds obvious now, doesn't it? If you wish to smack yourself in the forehead and curse loudly, you may proceed to do so. I can wait.

I ate another chip. Grandpa Smedry was supposed to have contacted me via the Courier's Lenses more than two hours before. It was getting late, even for him. I looked about, trying to determine if there were any Librarian agents in the airport crowd.

I couldn't spot any, but that didn't mean anything. I knew enough to realize that you can't always tell a Librarian by looking at one. While some dress the part — horn-rimmed glasses for the women, bow ties and vests for the men — others looked completely normal, blending in with the regular Hushlanders. Dangerous, but unseen. (Kind of like those troublemakers who read fantasy novels.)

I had a tough decision to make. I could continue wearing the Courier's Lenses, which would mark me as an Oculator to Librarian agents. Or, I could take them off, and thereby miss Grandpa Smedry's message when he got close enough to contact me.

If he got close enough to contact me.

A group of people walked over to where I was sitting, draping their luggage across several rows of chairs and chatting about the fog delays. I tensed, wondering if they were Librarian agents. Three months on the run had left me feeling anxious.

But that running was over. I would soon escape the Hushlands and finally get to visit my homeland. Nalhalla, one of the Free Kingdoms. A place that Hushlanders didn't even know existed, though it was a large continent that sat in the Pacific Ocean between North America and Asia.

I'd never seen it before, but I'd heard stories, and I'd seen some Free Kingdom technology. Cars that could drive themselves, hourglasses that could keep time no matter which direction you turned them. I longed to get to Nalhalla — though, even more desperately, I wanted to get out of Librarian-controlled lands.

Grandpa Smedry hadn't explained exactly *how* he planned to get me out, or even why we were meeting at the airport. It seemed unlikely that there would be any flights to the Free Kingdoms. However, no matter what the method, I knew our escape probably wouldn't be easy.

Fortunately, I had a few things on my side. First, I was an Oculator, and I had access to some fairly powerful Lenses. Second, I had my grandfather, who was an expert at avoiding Librarian agents. Third, I knew that the Librarians liked to keep a low profile, even while they secretly ruled most of the world. I probably didn't have to worry about police or airport security — the Librarians wouldn't want to involve them, for that would risk revealing the conspiracy to people who were too low ranked.

I also had my Talent. But . . . well, I wasn't really sure whether that was an advantage or not. It —

I froze. A man was standing in the waiting area of the gate next to mine. He was wearing a suit and sunglasses. And he was staring right at me. As soon as I noticed him, he turned away, looking too nonchalant.

Sunglasses probably meant Warrior's Lenses — one of the only kinds of Lenses that a non-Oculator could use. I stiffened; the man seemed to be muttering to himself.

Or talking into a radio receiver.

Shattering Glass! I thought, standing up and throwing on my backpack. I wove through the crowd, leaving the gate behind, and raised my hand to my eyes, intending to pull off the Courier's Lenses.

But . . . what if Grandpa Smedry tried to contact me? There was no way he'd be able to find me in the crowded airport. I needed to keep those Lenses on.

I feel I need to break the action here to warn you that I frequently break the action to mention trivial things. It's one of my bad habits that, along with wearing mismatched socks, tends to make people rather annoyed at me. It's not my fault, though, honestly. I blame society. (For the socks,

I mean. That breaking-the-action thing is *totally* my own fault.)

I hastened my pace, keeping my head down and my Lenses on. I hadn't gone far before I noticed a group of men in black suits and pink bow ties standing on a moving airport walkway a short distance ahead. They had several uniformed security guards with them.

I froze. *So much for not having to worry about the police. . . .* I tried to hold in my panic, turning — as covertly as I could — and hurrying in the other direction.

I should have realized that the rules would start changing. The Librarians had spent three months chasing Grandpa Smedry and me. They might hate the idea of involving local law enforcement, but they hated the idea of losing us even more.

A second group of Librarian agents were coming from the other direction. A good dozen warriors in Lenses, likely armed with glass swords and other advanced weapons. There was only one thing to do.

I stepped into the bathroom.

Numerous people were in there, doing their business. I rushed to the back wall. I let my backpack fall to the ground, then placed both hands against the wall's tiles.

A couple of men in the bathroom gave me odd looks, but I'd gotten used to those. People had given me odd looks for most of my life — what else would you expect for a kid who routinely broke things that weren't really that breakable? (Once, when I was seven, my Talent decided to break pieces of concrete as I stepped on them. I left a line of broken sidewalk squares behind me, like the footprints of some immense killer robot — one wearing size six sneakers.)

I closed my eyes, concentrating. Before, I'd let my Talent rule my life. I hadn't known that I could control it — I hadn't even been convinced that it was real.

Grandpa Smedry's arrival three months earlier had changed all of that. While dragging me off to infiltrate a Library and recover the Sands of Rashid, he'd helped me learn that I could *use* my Talent, rather than just be used by it.

I focused, and twin bursts of energy pulsed from my chest and down my arms. The tiles in front of me fell free, shattering as they hit the ground like a line of icicles knocked off of a railing. I continued to focus. People behind me cried out. The Librarians would be upon me any moment.

The entire wall broke, falling away from me. A water line began to spray into the air. I didn't pause to look behind at the shouting men, but instead reached back and grabbed my backpack.

The strap broke loose. I cursed quietly, grabbing the other one. It broke free too.

The Talent. Blessing and curse. I didn't let it rule me anymore — but I wasn't really in control either. It was as if the Talent and I had joint custody over my life; I got it on every other weekend and some holidays.

I left the backpack. I had my Lenses in the pockets of my jacket, and they were the only things of real value I owned. I leaped through the hole, scrambling over the rubble and into the bowels of the airport. (Hmm. Out of the bathroom and into the bowels — kind of opposite of the normal way.)

I was in some kind of service tunnel, poorly lit and even more poorly cleaned. I dashed down the tunnel for several minutes. I think I must have left the terminal behind, traveling through some access passageway to another building.

At the end, there were a few stairs leading to a large

door. I heard shouts behind me and risked a glance. A group of men were barreling down the passage toward me.

I spun and tugged on the doorknob. The door was locked, but doors have always been one of my specialties. The knob came off; I tossed it over my shoulder in an off-handed motion. Then I kicked the door open, bursting out into a large hangar.

Massive airplanes towered over me, their windshields dark. I hesitated, looking up at the enormous vehicles, feeling dwarfed as if by large beasts.

I shook myself out of the stupor. The Librarians were still behind me. Fortunately, it appeared as if this hangar was empty of people. I slammed the door, then placed my hand on the lock, using my Talent to break it so that the deadbolt jammed in place. I hopped over the railing and landed on a short line of steps leading down to the hangar's floor.

When I reached the bottom, my feet left tracks in the dusty floor. Fleeing out onto the runway seemed like an easy way to get myself arrested, considering the current state of airport security. However, hiding seemed risky as well.

That was a good metaphor for my life, actually. It seemed that no matter what I did, I ended up in even more danger than I'd been in before. One might have said that I constantly went "out of the frying pan and into the fire," which is a common Hushlands saying.

(Hushlanders, it might be noted, aren't very imaginative with their idioms. Personally, I say, "Out of the frying pan and into the deadly pit filled with sharks who are wielding chainsaws with killer kittens stapled to them." However, that one's having a rough time catching on.)

Fists began to bang on the door. I glanced at it, then made my decision. I'd try hiding.

I ran toward a small doorway on the floor of the hangar. It had slivers of light shining in around it, and I figured it led out onto the runway. I was careful to leave big, long footprints in the dust. Then — my false trail made — I hopped onto some boxes, moved across them, then jumped onto the ground.

The door shook as the men pounded. It wouldn't hold for long. I skidded down next to the wheel of a 747 and whipped off my Courier's Lenses. Then, I reached into my jacket. I had sewn a group of protective pockets onto the inside lining, and each one was cushioned with a special, Free Kingdoms material to protect the Lenses.

I pulled out a pair of green-Lensed spectacles and shoved them on.

The door burst.

I ignored it, instead focusing on the floor of the hangar. Then, I activated the Lenses. Immediately, a quick gust of wind blew from my face. It moved across the floor, erasing some of the footprints. Windstormer's Lenses, a gift from Grandpa Smedry the week after our first Librarian infiltration.

By the time the Librarians got through the door, cursing and muttering, only the footprints I *wanted* them to see were still there. I huddled down beside my wheel, holding my breath and trying to still my thumping heart as I heard a fleet of soldiers and policemen pile down the steps.

That's when I remembered my Firebringer's Lens.

I peeked up over the top of the 747 wheel. The Librarians had fallen for my trick and were moving along the floor toward the door out of the hangar. They weren't walking as quickly as I would have wanted, though, and several were glancing around with suspicious eyes.

I ducked back down before I could be spotted. My fingers felt the Firebringer's Lens — I only had one left — and I hesitantly brought it out. It was completely clear, with a single red dot in the center.

When activated, it shot forth a super-hot burst of energy, something like a laser. I could turn it on the Librarians. They had, after all, tried to kill me on several different occasions. They deserved it.

I sat for a moment, then quietly tucked the Lens back in its pocket and instead put my Courier's Lenses back on. If you've read the previous volume of this autobiography, you'll realize that I had some very particular ideas about heroism. A hero wasn't the type of person who turned a laser of pure energy upon the backs of a bunch of soldiers, particularly when that bunch included innocent security guards.

Sentiments like this one eventually got me into a lot of trouble. You probably remember how I'm going to end up; I mentioned it in the first book. I'll eventually be tied to an altar made from outdated encyclopedias, with cultists from the Librarian Order of the Shattered Lens preparing to spill my Oculator's blood in an unholy ceremony.

Heroism is what landed me there. Ironically, it also saved my life that day in the airport hangar. You see, if I hadn't put on my Courier's Lenses, I would have missed what happened next.

Alcatraz? a voice suddenly asked in my mind.

The voice nearly made me cry out in surprise.

Uh, Alcatraz? Hello? Is anyone listening?

The voice was fuzzy and indistinct, and it wasn't the voice of my grandfather. However, it *was* coming from the Courier's Lenses.

Oh, bother! the voice said. *Um. I've never been good with Courier's Lenses.*

It faded in and out, as if someone were speaking through a radio that wasn't getting good reception. It wasn't Grandpa Smedry, but at that moment, I was willing to take a chance on whoever it was.

"I'm here!" I whispered, activating the Lenses.

A blurry face fuzzed into existence in front of me, hovering like a hologram in the air. It belonged to a young girl with dark tan skin and black hair.

Hello? she asked. *Is someone there? Can you talk louder or something?*

"Not really," I hissed, glancing out at the Librarians. Most of them had moved out the door, but a small group of men had apparently been assigned to search the hangar. Mostly security guards.

Um . . . okay, the voice said. *Uh, who is this?*

"Who do you think it is?" I asked in annoyance. "I'm Alcatraz. Who are you?"

Oh, I — the image, and voice, fuzzed for a moment — *sent to pick you up. Sorry! Uh, where are you?*

"In a hangar," I said. One of the guards perked up, then pulled out a gun, pointing it in my direction. He'd heard me.

"Shattering Glass!" I hissed, ducking back down.

You really shouldn't swear like that, you know . . . , the girl said.

"Thanks," I hissed as quietly as possible. "Who are you, and how are you going to get me out of this?"

There was a pause. A dreadful, terrible, long, annoying, frustrating, deadly, nerve-racking, incredibly wordy pause.

I . . . don't really know, the girl said. *I — wait just a second. Bastille says that you should run out somewhere in the open, then signal us. It's too foggy down there. We can't really see much.*

Down there? I thought. Still, if Bastille was with this girl, that seemed like a good sign. Although Bastille would probably chastise me for getting myself into so much trouble, she did have a habit of being very effective at what she did. Hopefully that would include rescuing me.

"Hey!" a voice said. I turned to the side, staring out at one of the guards. "I found someone!"

Time to break some things, I thought, taking a deep breath. Then I sent a burst of breaking power into the wheel of the airplane.

I ducked away, leaping to my feet as lug nuts popped free from the airplane wheel. The guard raised his gun but didn't fire.

"Shoot him!" said a man in a black suit, the Librarian who stood directing things from the side of the room.

"I'm not shooting a *kid*," the guard said. "Where are these terrorists you were talking about?"

Good man, I thought as I dashed toward the front of the hangar. At that moment, the wheel of the airplane fell completely off, and the entire front of the vehicle crashed down against the pavement. Men cried out in surprise, and the security guards dived for cover.

The Librarian in black grabbed a handgun from one of the confused guards and pointed it at me. I just smiled.

The gun, of course, fell apart as soon as the Librarian pulled the trigger. My Talent protects me when it can — and the more moving parts a weapon has, the easier it is to break. I rammed my shoulder into the massive hangar doors and sent a shock of breaking power into them. Screws and nuts and bolts fell like rain around me, hitting the ground. Several guards peeked out from behind boxes.

The entire front of the hangar came off, falling away from me and hitting the ground outside with a reverberating crash. I hesitated, shocked, even though that was exactly what I'd wanted to happen. Swirling fog began to creep into the hangar around me.

It seemed that my Talent was getting even more powerful. Before, I'd broken things like pots and dishes, with the very rare exception of something larger, like the concrete I had broken when I was seven. That was *nothing* like what I'd been doing lately: taking the wheels off of airplanes and making entire hangar doors fall off. Not for the first time, I wondered just how much I could break if I really needed to.

And how much the Talent could break if *it* decided that it wanted to.

There wasn't time to contemplate that, as the Librarians outside had noticed the ruckus. They stood, black upon the noonday fog, looking back at me. Most of them had spread out to the sides, and so the only way for me to go was straight ahead.

I dashed out onto the wet tarmac, running for all I was worth. The Librarians began to yell, and several tried — completely ineffectively — to fire guns at me. They should have known better. In their defense, few people — even Librarians — are accustomed to dealing with a Smedry as powerful as I was. Against others, they might have been able to get off a few shots before something went wrong. Firearms aren't *completely* useless in the Free Kingdoms, they're just much less powerful.

The shooting — or lack thereof — bought me just a few seconds of time. Unfortunately, there were a pair of Librarians in my path.

"Get ready!" I yelled into my Courier's Lenses. Then I whipped them off and put on the Windstormer's Lenses. I focused as hard as I could, blowing forth a burst of wind from my eyes. Both Librarians were knocked to the ground, and I leaped over them.

Other Librarians cried out from behind, chasing me as I moved out onto a runway. Puffing, I reached into a pocket and pulled free my Firebringer's Lens. I spun and activated the Lens.

It started to glow. The group of Librarians pulled to a halt. They knew enough to recognize that Lens. I held it out, then pointed it up into the air. It shot a line of red firelight upward, piercing the fog.

That had better be enough of a signal, I thought. The Librarians gathered together, obviously preparing to rush at me, Lens or no Lens. I prepared my Windstormer's Lenses, hoping I could use them to blow the Librarians back long enough for Bastille to save me.

The Librarians, however, did not charge. I stood, anxious, the Firebringer's Lens still firing into the air. What were they waiting for?

The Librarians parted, and a dark figure — silhouetted in the muggy fog — moved through them. I couldn't see much, but something about this figure was just plain *wrong*. It was a head taller than the others, and one of its arms was several feet longer than the other. Its head was misshapen. Perhaps inhuman. Most definitely dangerous.

I shivered, taking an involuntary step backward. The dark figure raised its bony arm, as if pointing a gun.

I'll be all right, I told myself. *Guns are useless against me.*

There was a crack in the air, then the Firebringer's Lens exploded in my fingers, hit square on by the creature's bullet. I yelled, pulling my hand down.

Shoot my Lens rather than me. This one is more clever than the others.

The dark figure walked forward, and part of me wanted to wait to see just what it was that made this creature's arm and head so misshapen. The rest of me was just plain horrified. The figure started to run, and that was enough. I did the smart thing (I'm capable of that on occasion) and dashed away as quickly as I could.

Instantly, I seemed to be pulled backward. The wind whistled in my ears oddly, and each step felt far more difficult than it should have. I began to sweat, and soon it was tough to even walk.

Something was very, very wrong. As I continued to move, forcing myself on despite the strange force towing me backward, I began to think that I could *feel* the dark thing behind me. I could sense it, twisted and vile, getting closer and closer.

I could barely move. Each. Step. Got. Tougher.

A rope ladder slapped down against the tarmac a short distance in front of me. I cried out and lunged for it, grabbing ahold. My weight must have told those above that I was on board, because the ladder suddenly jerked upward, towing me with it and ripping me free from whatever force had been holding me back. I felt the pressure lighten, and glancing down, I let out a relieved breath.

The figure still stood there, indistinct in the fog, only a few feet from where I'd been. It stared up as I was lifted to safety, until the ground and the creature disappeared into the fog.

I let out a sigh of relief, relaxing against the wood and rope. A few moments later, my ladder and I were pulled free from the fog, bursting out into open air.

I looked up and saw perhaps the most awesome sight I'd ever seen in my entire life.

CHAPTER 2

This is the second book of the series. Those of you who have read the first book can skip this introduction and move on. The rest of you, stay put.

I'd like to congratulate you on finding this book. I'm glad you're reading a serious work about real world politics, rather than wasting your time on something silly like a fantasy book about a fictional character like Napoleon. (Either Napoleon, actually. They both have something to do, in their own way, with being Blownapart.)

Now, I do have to admit something. I find it very disturbing that you readers have decided to begin with the *second* book in the series. That's a very bad habit to have — worse, even, than wearing mismatched socks. In fact, on the bad-habit scale, it ranks somewhere between chewing with your mouth open and making quacking noises when your friends are trying to study. (Try that one some time — it's really fun.)

It's because of people like you that we authors have to clog our second books with all kinds of explanations. We have to, essentially, invent the wheel again — or at least renew our patent.

You should already know who I am, and you should understand Oculatory Lenses and Smedry Talents. With all of that knowledge, you could easily understand the events that led me to the point where I hung dangling from a rope ladder, staring up at something awesome that I haven't yet described.

Why don't I just describe it now? Well, by asking that question, you prove that you haven't read the first book. Let me explain by using a brief object lesson.

Do you remember the first chapter of this book? (I certainly hope that you do, since it was only a few pages back.) What did I promise you there? I promised that I was going to stop using cliff-hangers and other frustrating storytelling practices. Now, what did I do at the end of that very same chapter? I left you with a frustrating cliff-hanger, of course.

That was intended to teach you something: That I'm completely trustworthy and would never dare lie to you. At least not more than, oh, half a dozen times per chapter.

I dangled from the rope ladder, wind whipping at my jacket, heart still pounding from my escape. Flying above me was an enormous glass dragon.

Perhaps you've seen a dragon depicted in art or cinema. I certainly have. However, looking up at the thing above me in the air, I knew that the images I'd seen in films were only approximations. Those movies tended to make dragons — even the threatening ones — seem bulbous, with large stomachs and awkward wingspans.

The reptilian form above me was nothing like that. There was an incredible sleekness to it, snakelike but at the same time powerful. It had three sets of wings running down the length of its body, and they flapped in harmony. I could see six legs as well — all tucked up underneath the slender body — and it had a long glass tail whipping behind it in the air.

Its triangular head twisted about — translucent glass sparkling — and looked at me. It was angular, with sharp lines, like an arrowhead. And there were people standing in its eyeball.

This isn't a creature at all, I realized, hanging desperately to the ladder. *But a vehicle. One crafted completely from glass!*

"Alcatraz!" a voice called from above, barely audible over the sound of the wind.

I glanced up. The ladder led into an open section of the dragon's stomach. A familiar face was poking out of the hole, looking down at me. The same age as I am, Bastille had long, silver hair that whipped in the wind. The last time I'd seen her, she'd gone with two of my cousins into hiding. Grandpa Smedry had worried that keeping us all together was making us easier to track.

She said something, but it was lost in the wind.

"What?" I yelled.

"I *said*," she yelled, "are you going to climb up here, or do you intend to hang there looking stupid for the entire trip?"

That's Bastille for you. She did kind of have a point, though. I climbed up the swinging ladder — which was much harder and much more nerve-racking than you might think.

I forced myself onward. It would have been a pretty stupid end to get lifted to safety at the last moment, then drop off the ladder and squish against the ground below. When I got close enough, Bastille gave me a hand and helped me up into the dragon's belly. She pulled a glass lever on the wall, and the ladder began to retract.

I watched, curious. At that point in my life, I hadn't really seen much silimatic technology, and I still considered it all to be "magic." There was no noise as the ladder came up — no clinking of gears or hum of a motor. The ladder just wound around a turning wheel.

A glass plate slid over the open hole in the floor. Around me, glass walls sparkled in the sunlight, completely transparent. The view was amazing — we'd already moved beyond the fog — and I could see the landscape below, extending in all directions. I almost felt as if I were hovering in the sky, alone, in the beautiful serenity of —

"You done gawking yet?" Bastille snapped, arms folded.

I shot her a glance. "Excuse me," I said, "but I'm trying to have a beautiful moment here."

She snorted. "What are you going to do? Write a poem? Come on." With that, she began to walk along the glass hallway inside the dragon, moving toward the head. I smiled wryly to myself. I hadn't seen Bastille in over two months, and neither of us had known if the other would even survive long enough to meet up again.

But, where Bastille is concerned, that was actually a nice reception. She didn't throw anything at me, hit me with anything, or even swear at me. Rather heartwarming.

I rushed to catch up with her. "What happened to your business suit?"

She looked down. Instead of wearing her stylish jacket and slacks, she was dressed in a much more stiff, militaristic costume. Black with silver buttons, it looked kind of like the dress uniforms that military personnel wear on formal occasions. It even had those little metal things on the shoulders that I can never remember how to spell.

"We're not in the Hushlands anymore, Smedry," she said. "Or, at least, we soon won't be. So why wear their clothing?"

"I thought you liked those clothes."

She shrugged. "It's my place to wear this now. Besides, I like wearing a glassweave jacket, and this uniform has one."

I *still* haven't figured out how they make clothing out of glass. It's apparently very expensive but worth the cost. A glassweave jacket could take quite a beating, protecting its wearer almost as well as a suit of armor. Back in the Library infiltration we'd done, Bastille had survived a blow that really should have killed her.

"All right," I said. "What about this thing we're flying in? I assume it's some sort of vehicle and not really a living creature?"

Bastille gave me one of her barely tolerant looks. I keep telling her she should trademark those. She could sell photos of herself making the face so that people could use them to scare children, turn milk into curds, or frighten terrorists into surrendering.

She doesn't find comments like that very funny.

"Of *course* it's not alive," she said. "Alivening things is Dark Oculary, as I believe you've been told."

"Okay, but why make it in the shape of a dragon?"

"What should we do?" Bastille said. "Build our aircraft in the shapes of . . . long tubey contraptions, or whatever it is those airplanes look like? I can't believe they stay in the air. Their wings can't even flap!"

"They don't need to flap. They have jet engines!"

"Oh, and then why do they have wings?"

I paused. "Something about airlift and physics and stuff like that."

Bastille snorted again. "Physics," she muttered. "A Librarian scam."

"Physics isn't a scam, Bastille. It's very logical."

"Librarian logic."

"Facts."

"Oh?" she asked. "And if they're facts, then why are they so complicated? Shouldn't explanations about the natural world be simple? Why is there all of that needless math and complexity?" She shook her head, turning away from me. "All of that is just intended to confuse people. If the Hushlanders think that science is too complicated to understand, then they'll be too afraid to ask questions."

She eyed me, obviously watching to see if I would continue the argument. I did not. There was one thing about hanging around with Bastille — it was teaching me when to hold my tongue. Even if I didn't hold my brain.

How does she know so much about what the Librarians teach in their schools? I thought. *She knows an awful lot about my people.*

Bastille was still an enigma to me. She'd wanted to be an Oculator when she was younger, so she knew quite a bit about Lenses. However, I still couldn't quite figure out why she'd even wanted to be one so badly in the first place. Everyone — or, well, everyone outside the Hushlands — knows that Oculatory powers are hereditary. One can't just "become" an Oculator in the same way one can choose to become a lawyer, an accountant, or a potted plant.

Either way, I was finding it increasingly disconcerting to be able to see through the floor, particularly when we were so high up. The motions of the giant vehicle didn't help either. Now that I was inside of it, I could see that the dragon was made of glass plates that slid together such that the entire thing could move and twist. Each flap of the wings made the body undulate around me.

We reached the head, which I assumed was the dragon's version of a cockpit. The glass door slid open. I stepped up onto a maroon carpet — thankfully obscuring my view of the ground — and was met by two people.

Neither of them was my grandfather. *Where is he?* I wondered with growing annoyance. Bastille, strangely, took up position next to the doorway, standing with a stiff back and staring straight ahead.

One of the people turned toward me. "Lord Smedry," the woman said, standing with arms straight at her sides. She had on a suit of steel plate armor, like what I'd seen in museums. Except this armor seemed a lot better fitting. The pieces bent together in a more flexible manner, and the metal itself was thinner.

The woman bowed her head to me, helmet under her arm, her hair a deep, metallic silver. The face seemed familiar. I glanced at Bastille, then back at the woman.

"You're Bastille's mother?" I asked.

"I am indeed, Lord Smedry," the woman said, the tone of her voice as stiff as her armor. "I am —"

"Oh, Alcatraz!" the other person said, interrupting the woman. This girl sat in the chair beside the dash of the cockpit, and she wore a pink tunic with brown trousers. She had the face I'd seen through the Courier's Lenses — long black hair, a little bit curly, with dark skin and slightly plump features.

"I'm so glad you made it," the girl exclaimed. "For a while, I thought we'd lost you! Then Bastille saw that light shooting into the air, and we figured it was from you. It seems that we were right!"

"And you are . . . ?" I asked.

"Australia Smedry!" she said, hopping out of her chair and rushing over to give me a hug. "Your cousin, silly! Sing's sister."

"Gak!" I said, nearly being crushed by the powerful hug. Bastille's mother looked on, arms crossed behind her back in a kind of parade-rest sort of pose.

Australia finally let me go. She was probably around sixteen, and she had on a pair of blue Lenses.

"You're an Oculator!" I said.

"Of course I am!" she said. "How else do you think I contacted you? I'm not really that good with these Lenses. Or . . . um, most Lenses, actually. Anyway, it's so wonderful to meet you, finally! I've heard a lot about you. Well, a couple of things really. Okay, so only two letters from Sing, but they were *very* complimentary. Do you really have the Talent of Breaking Things?"

I shrugged. "That's what they tell me. What's your Talent?"

Australia smiled. "I can wake up in the morning looking incredibly ugly!"

"Oh . . . how wonderful." I still wasn't certain how to respond to Smedry Talents. I usually couldn't ever tell if the person telling me was excited or disappointed by the power.

Australia, it seemed, was excited by pretty much everything. She nodded perkily. "I know. It's a fun Talent — nothing like breaking things — but I make it work for me!" She glanced about. "I wonder where Kaz went. He'll want to meet you too."

"Another cousin?"

"Your uncle, actually," Australia said. "Your father's brother. He was just here. . . . Must have wandered off again."

I sensed another Talent. "His Smedry ability is to get lost?"

Australia smiled. "You've heard of him!"

I shook my head. "Lucky guess."

"He'll show up eventually — he always does. Anyway, I'm just *so* excited to meet you!"

I nodded hesitantly.

"Lady Smedry," Bastille's mother said from behind. "I do not intend to give offense, but shouldn't you be flying the *Dragonaut*?"

"Gak!" Australia said, hopping back into her seat. She put her hand onto a glowing square on the front of what appeared to be a glass control panel.

I walked up beside her, looking out through the dragon's eye. We were still moving upward and soon would enter the clouds.

"So," I said, glancing back at Bastille. "Where's Grandpa?"

Bastille remained silent, staring ahead, back stiff.

"Bastille?"

"You should not address her, Lord Smedry," Bastille's mother said. "She's only here acting as my squire, and is currently beneath your notice."

"That's nonsense! She's my friend."

Bastille's mother didn't respond to that, though I caught a slight look of disapproval in her eyes. She immediately stiffened, as if having noticed that I was studying her.

"Squire Bastille has been stripped of her rank, Lord Smedry," Bastille's mother said. "You should address all of your questions to me, as I will be acting as your Knight of Crystallia from now on."

Great, I thought.

I should note here that Bastille's mother — Draulin — is by no means as stiff and boring a person as she might at first seem. I have it on good authority that once, about ten years ago, she was heard to laugh, though some still claim it was a particularly nasty sneeze. She has also been known to blink occasionally, though only on her lunch break.

"Squire Bastille has not executed her duty in a manner befitting one who carries the title Knight of Crystallia," Draulin continued. "She performed in a sloppy, embarrassing manner that endangered not one, but *both* Oculators under her protection. She allowed herself to be captured. She allowed a member of the Conclave of Kings to be tortured by a Dark Oculator. And, on top of all of that, she lost her bonded Crystin sword."

I glanced at Bastille, who still stared straight ahead, jaw clenched tightly. I felt anger rise in me.

"None of that was her fault," I said, looking back at Draulin. "You can't punish her for it! *I'm* the one who broke her sword."

"It isn't fault that is punished," Draulin said, "but failure. This is the decision of the Crystin leaders, Lord Smedry, and I was sent to deliver it. The judgment will stand. As you know, the Crystin are outside the jurisdiction of any kingdom or royal line."

Actually, I didn't know that. I didn't know a whole lot about Crystallia in the first place. I'd barely even gotten used to being called "Lord Smedry." I had come to understand that Smedries are held in great respect by most Free Kingdomers, and figured that my title was something of a term of affection for them.

There was, of course, a lot more to it than that. But, there always is, isn't there?

I glanced back at Bastille, where she stood at the back of the cockpit, face red. *I need to talk to my grandfather,* I decided. *He can help sort this out.*

I sat down in the chair beside Australia. "All right, where's my grandfather?"

Australia glanced at me, then blushed. "We're not exactly sure. We got a note from him this morning — delivered via Transcriber's Lenses. It told us what to do. I can show you the note, if you want."

"Please," I said.

Australia fished in her tunic for a moment, searching through pockets. Finally, she found a wrinkled-up piece of paper and handed it over to me.

Australia, it read.

> I don't know if I'll be there at the pickup point. Something has come up that requires my attention. Kindly fetch my grandson for me, as planned,

and take him to Nalhalla. I will meet up with you
when I can.

Leavenworth Smedry.

Outside, we rose into the clouds. The vehicle really seemed to be picking up speed.

"So, we're going to Nalhalla?" I asked, glancing back at Bastille's mother.

"As long as that's what you command," the woman said. Her tone implied it was really the only choice.

"I guess it is, then," I said, feeling a slight disappointment, the reason for which I couldn't pin down.

"You should go to your quarters, Lord Smedry," Draulin said. "You can rest there; it will take several hours to journey across the ocean to Nalhalla."

"Very well," I said, rising.

"I will lead you," Draulin said.

"Nonsense," I said, glancing at Bastille. "Have the squire do it."

"As you command," the knight said, nodding her head at Bastille. I walked from the cockpit, Bastille trailing behind, then waited until the door slid closed. Through its glass, I could see Draulin turn and stand, still at parade rest, facing out the eyeball of the dragon.

I turned to Bastille. "What's *that* all about?"

She flushed. "Just what she said, Smedry. Come on. I'll take you to your room."

"Oh, don't get like that with me," I said, rushing to catch up. "You lose one sword, and they bust you back to squire? That doesn't make any sense."

Bastille flushed even more deeply. "My mother is a very brave and well-respected Knight of Crystallia. She always does what is best for the order and never acts without careful thought."

"That doesn't answer my question."

Bastille glanced down. "Look, I told you when I lost my sword that I would be in trouble. Well, see, I'm in trouble. I'll deal with it. I don't need your pity."

"It isn't pity! It's annoyance." I eyed her. "What aren't you telling me, Bastille?"

Bastille muttered something about Smedries but otherwise gave no response. She stalked through the glass corridors, leading me toward — I assumed — my cabin.

As I walked, however, I grew more and more displeased with events. Grandpa Smedry must have discovered something, otherwise he wouldn't have missed the pickup, and I hated feeling like I was being left out of important things.

Now, this is a stupid way to feel, if you think about it. I was *always* being left out of important things. At that very moment, there were thousands of people doing very important things all across the world — everything from getting married to jumping out windows — and I wasn't a part of any of it. The truth is, even the most important people get left out of most things that happen in the world.

But I was still annoyed. As I walked, I realized I still had on my Courier's Lenses. They were very limited in range, but maybe Grandfather was close by.

I activated the Lenses. *Grandfather?* I thought, focusing. *Grandfather, are you there?*

Nothing. I sighed. It had been a long shot anyway. I didn't really —

A very faint image appeared in front of me. *Alcatraz?* a distant voice said.

Grandfather? I thought, growing excited. *Yes, it's me!*

Flustered Farlands! How did you contact me across such a distance? The voice was so weak that I could barely hear it, even though it was speaking directly into my mind.

Grandfather, where are you?

The voice said something, but was too soft to hear. I focused harder, closing my eyes. *Grandfather!*

Alcatraz! I think I've found your father. He came here. I'm sure of it!

Where, Grandfather? I asked.

The voice was growing even fainter. *The Library . . .*

Grandfather! What Library?

Library . . . of Alexandria . . .

And then he was gone. I concentrated, but the voice didn't come back. Finally, I sighed, opening my eyes.

"You all right, Smedry?" Bastille asked, giving me a strange look.

"The Library of Alexandria," I said. "Where is it?"

Bastille eyed me. "Um, in Alexandria?"

Right. "Where is that?"

"Egypt."

"Like, the real Egypt? My Egypt?"

Bastille shrugged. "Yeah, I think so. Why?"

I glanced back toward the cockpit.

"No," Bastille said, folding her arms. "Alcatraz, I know what you're thinking. We're *not* going there."

"Why not?"

"The Library of Alexandria is extremely dangerous. Even regular Librarians are scared to go into it. Nobody in their right mind ever visits that place."

"That sounds about right," I said. "Because Grandpa Smedry is there right now."

"How would you know something like that?"

I tapped my Lenses.

"They wouldn't work at such a distance."

"They did. I just talked to him. He's there, Bastille." *And . . . he thinks my father is too.*

That gave me a twist in my stomach. I'd grown up assuming that both of my parents were dead. Now I was beginning to think that both were actually alive. My mother was a Librarian and worked for the wrong side. I wasn't entirely sure I wanted to know what my father was like.

No. That's wrong. I *really* wanted to know what my father was like. I was just afraid of it at the same time.

I glanced back at Bastille.

"You're sure he's there?" she asked.

I nodded.

"Shattering Glass," she muttered. "Last time we tried something like this, you almost got killed, your grandfather got tortured, and I lost my sword. Do we *really* want to go through that again?"

"What if he's in trouble?"

"He's *always* in trouble," Bastille said.

We fell silent. Then, both of us turned and rushed back to the cockpit.

CHAPTER 3

I'd like to make something clear. I have been unfair to you. That is to be expected, liar that I am.

In the first book of this series, I made some sweeping generalizations about librarians, many of which are not completely true.

I need to come clean. There are several kinds of librarians. There are the ones that I talked about in my last book — the Librarians, with a capital L. We also call them the Librarians of Biblioden, or the Scrivener's Librarians. Most of what I said about that particular group is, indeed, factual.

However, I didn't take the time to explain that they're not the *only* kind of librarians. You may, therefore, have assumed that all librarians are evil cultists who want to take over the world, enslave humanity, and sacrifice people on their altars.

This is completely untrue. Not all librarians are evil cultists. Some librarians are instead vengeful undead who want to suck your soul.

I'm glad we cleared that up.

"You want to do *what*?" Bastille's mother demanded.

"Fly to the Library of Alexandria," I said.

"Out of the question, my lord. We can't possibly do that."

"We have to," I said.

Australia turned toward me, leaving one hand on the glowing glass square that allowed her, somehow, to pilot the *Dragonaut.* "Alcatraz, why would you want to go to Alexandria? It's not a very friendly place."

"Grandpa Smedry is there," I said. "That means we need to go too."

"He didn't say he was going to Egypt," Australia said, glancing again at the crumpled note that he'd sent.

"The Library of Alexandria is one of the most dangerous places in the Hushlands, Lord Smedry," Draulin continued. "Most regular Librarians will only kill or imprison you. The Curators of Alexandria, however, will steal your soul. I cannot, in good conscience, allow you to be placed in such danger."

The tall, armored woman still stood with her arms behind her back. She kept her silver hair long but in a utilitarian ponytail, and she did not meet my eyes, but instead stared directly forward.

Now, I'd like to point out that what I did next was completely logical. Really. There's a law of the universe — unfamiliar to most people in the Hushlands but quite commonly known to Free Kingdoms scientists. It is called the Law of Inevitable Occurrence.

In simple layman's terms, this law states that some things just *have* to happen. If there's a red button on a console with the words DON'T PUSH taped above it, someone will push it. If there's a gun hanging conspicuously above Chekhov's fireplace, someone is going to end up shooting it (probably at Nietzsche).

And if there's a stern woman telling you what to do — yet at the same time calling you "my lord" — you're going to just have to figure out how far you can push her.

"Jump up and down on one foot," I said, pointing at Draulin.

"Excuse me?" she asked, flushing.

"Do it. That's an order."

And she did, looking rather annoyed.

"You can stop," I said.

She did so. "Would you mind telling me what that was about, Lord Smedry?"

"Well, I wanted to figure out if you'd do what I commanded."

"Of course I will," Draulin said. "As the oldest child of Attica Smedry, you are the heir to the pure Smedry line. You outrank both your cousin and your uncle, which means you are in command of this vessel."

"Wonderful," I said. "So that means I can decide where we go, right?"

Bastille's mother fell silent. "Well," she finally said, "that is technically true, my lord. However, I have been charged with safely bringing you back to Nalhalla. Asking me to take you to such a dangerous location would be foolhardy, and —"

"Yeah, that's just spiffy," I said. "Australia, let's get going. I want to be in Egypt as soon as possible."

Bastille's mother closed her mouth, growing even more red in the face. Australia just shrugged and reached over to put her hand on another glass square. "Um, take us to the Library of Alexandria," she said.

The giant glass dragon shifted slightly, beginning to undulate in a different direction, six wings flapping in succession.

"That's it?" I asked.

Australia nodded. "It'll still take us a few hours to get there, though. We'll fly up over the pole and down into the Middle East, rather than out toward Nalhalla."

"Well, good, then," I said, feeling a little anxious as I realized what I'd done. Only a short time back, I'd been eager to get to safety. Now I was determined to head to a place that everyone else was telling me was insanely, ridiculously dangerous?

What was I doing? What business did I have taking command and giving orders? Feeling self-conscious, I left the cockpit again. Bastille trailed along behind me. "I'm not sure why I did that," I confessed as we walked.

"Your grandfather might be in danger."

"Yeah, but what are *we* going to do about it?"

"We helped him in the last Library infiltration," she said. "Saved him from Blackburn."

I fell silent, walking down the glass corridor. Yes, we had saved Grandpa Smedry . . . but . . . well, something told me that Grandpa Smedry would have gotten away from Blackburn eventually. The old Smedry had lived for more than a century, and — from what I understood — had managed to wiggle out of plenty of predicaments far worse than that one.

He'd been the one to fight Blackburn with the Lenses — I'd been helpless. True, I'd managed to break the Firebringer's Lens and trick Blackburn in the end. But I hadn't really known what I was doing. My victories seemed more like happenstance than they did anything else. And now I was heading into danger yet again?

Nevertheless, it was done. The *Dragonaut* had changed course, and we were on our way. *We'll look around outside the place,* I thought. *If it looks too dangerous, we don't have to go in.*

I was about to explain this decision to Bastille when a sudden voice spoke from behind us. "Bastille! We've changed course. What's that all about?"

I turned in shock. A short man, perhaps four feet tall, was walking down the corridor toward us. He most certainly hadn't been there before, and I couldn't figure out where he'd come from.

The man wore rugged clothing: a leather jacket, his tunic tucked into sturdy pants, a pair of boots. He had a wide face with a broad chin and dark, curly hair.

"A fairy!" I said immediately.

The short man stopped, looking confused. "That's a new one," he noted.

"What kind are you?" I asked. "Leprechaun? Elf?"

The short man raised an eyebrow, then glanced at Bastille. "Hazelnuts, Bastille," he swore. "Who's *this* clown?"

"Kaz, this is your nephew Alcatraz."

The short man glanced back at me. "Oh . . . I see. He seems a bit more dense than I assumed he'd be."

I flushed. "You're . . . not a fairy, then?"

He shook his head.

"Are you a dwarf? Like in *Lord of the Rings*?"

He shook his head.

"You're just a . . . midget?"

He regarded me with a flat stare. "You realize that *midget* isn't a good term to use, don't you? Even most Hushlanders know that. Midgets are what people used to call my kind when they stuck us in freak shows."

I paused. "What should I call you, then?"

"Well, Kaz is preferable. Kazan is my full name, though the blasted Librarians finally named a prison that a while back."

Bastille nodded. "In Russia."

The short man sighed. "Regardless, if you absolutely *have* to reference my height, I generally think that *short person* works just fine. Anyway, is someone going to explain why we changed course?"

I was still too busy being embarrassed to answer. I hadn't intended to insult my uncle. (Fortunately, I've gotten much better at this over the years. I'm now quite good at insulting people intentionally, and I can even do it in languages you Free Kingdomers don't speak. So there, you dagblad.)

Thankfully, Bastille spoke up and answered Kaz's question. "We got word that your father is at the Library of Alexandria. We think he might be in trouble."

"So we're heading there?" Kaz asked.

Bastille nodded.

Kaz perked up. "Wonderful!" he said. "Finally, some good news on this trip."

"Wait," I said. "That's *good* news?"

"Of course it is! I've wanted to explore that place for decades. Never could find a good enough excuse. I'll go get preparing!" He took off down the corridor toward the cockpit.

"Kaz?" Bastille called. He stopped, glancing back.

"Your room is that way." She pointed down a side corridor.

"Coconuts," he swore under his breath. Then, he headed the way she'd indicated.

"That's right," I said. "His Talent. Getting lost."

Bastille nodded. "What's worse is that he generally acts as our guide."

"How does *that* work?"

"Oddly," she said, continuing down the corridor.

I sighed. "I don't think he likes me very much."

"You seem to have that effect on people when they first meet you. I didn't like you very much at first either." She eyed me. "Still not sure if that's changed or not."

"You're so kind." As we walked down the dragon's snake-like body, I noticed a large glow coming from between the shoulder blades of a pair of wings above. The glass here sparkled and shifted, as if there were a lot of surfaces and delicate parts moving about. At the center of the mass was a deep, steady glow — like a smoldering fire. The light was being shaded by occasional moving pieces of glass that weren't translucent. So, every few seconds, the light would grow darker — then grow brighter again.

I pointed up. "What's that?"

"The engine," Bastille said.

There weren't any of the noises I had come to associate with a running motor — no hum, no moving pistons, no burning fire. Not even any steam. "How does it work?"

Bastille shrugged. "I'm no silimatic engineer."

"You're no Oculator, either," I noted. "But you know enough about Lenses to surprise most people."

"That's because I *studied* Lenses. Never did care much about silimatics. Come on. Do you want to get to your room or not?"

I did, and I was tired, so I let her lead me away. Turns out, actually, that silimatic engines aren't really that complex. They're actually a fair bit more easy to understand than regular Hushlander engines.

It all involves a special kind of sand, named brightsand, which gives off a glow when it's heated. That light then causes certain types of glass to do strange things. Some will rise into the air when exposed to silimatic light, others will drop downward when exposed to it. So, all you have to do is control which glass sees the light at which time, and you've got an engine.

I know you Hushlanders probably find that ridiculous. You ask yourselves, "If sand is that valuable, why is it so commonplace?" You are, of course, the victims of a terrible conspiracy. (Don't you ever get tired of that?)

The Librarians take great pains to make people ignore sand. They have, at great expense, flooded the Hushlands with dullsand — one of the few types of sand that doesn't really do anything at all, even when you melt it. What better way is there to make people ignore something than to make it seem commonplace?

Don't even get me started on the economic value of belly-button lint.

We finally reached my quarters. The body of the dragon-snake was a good twenty feet wide, so there was plenty of room along its length for rooms. I noticed, however, that all of the walls were translucent.

"Not a lot of privacy here, is there?" I asked.

Bastille rolled her eyes, then placed her hand on a

panel on the side of the wall. "Dark," she said. The wall immediately grew black. She glanced back at me. "We had it on translucent so that it would be easier to hide from people."

"Oh," I said. "So, this is technology and not magic?"

"Of course it is. Anyone can do it, after all. Not just Oculators."

"But Australia is the one flying the dragon."

"That's not because she's an Oculator, it's because she's a pilot. Look, I've got to get back to the cockpit. My mother's going to be angry at me for taking so long."

I glanced back at her. It seemed like something was really bothering her. "I'm sorry I broke your sword," I said.

She shrugged. "I didn't ever really deserve it in the first place."

"Why do you say that?"

"Everyone knows it," Bastille said, her voice betraying more than a little bitterness. "Even my mother felt that I should never have been dubbed a full knight. She didn't think that I was ready."

"She sure is stern."

"She hates me."

I looked over at her, shocked. "Bastille! I'm sure she doesn't hate you. She's your mother."

"She's ashamed of me," Bastille said. "Always has been. But . . . I don't know why I'm talking to *you* about this. Go take a nap, Smedry. Leave the important things to people who know what they're doing."

With that, she stalked away, heading back toward the cockpit. I sighed, but pulled open the glass door and walked into the room. There was no bed, though I did find a rolled-up mattress in the corner. The room, like the rest of the dragon, undulated up and down, each flap of the wings sending a ripple down the entire length of the body.

It had been a bit sickening at first, but I was getting used to it. I sat down, staring out the glass wall of my room. It was still transparent — Bastille had only made the one behind me black.

Clouds spread out below me, extending into the distance, white and lumpy, like the landscape of some alien planet — or perhaps like mashed potatoes that hadn't been whipped quite long enough. The sun, setting in the distance, was a brilliant yellow pat of butter, slowly melting as it disappeared.

As that analogy might have indicated, I was getting a bit hungry.

Still, I was safe. And I was finally free. Out of the Hushlands, ready to begin my journey to the lands where I'd been born. True, we'd stop in Egypt to pick up my grandfather, but I still felt relieved to be moving.

I was on my way. On my way to find my father, perhaps on my way to discover who I really was.

I'd eventually realize I didn't like what I found. But, for the moment, I felt good. And — despite the glass beneath me showing a drop straight down, despite my hunger, despite our destination — I found myself feeling relaxed. I drifted off, curling up on the mattress and falling asleep.

I woke up when a missile exploded a few feet from my head.

CHAPTER 4

You think you've figured it out, have you? My logical dilemma? My argumentative lapse? My brain freeze of rationality? My . . . uh . . . traffic jam of lucidity?

Let's just forget that last one.

Anyway, there is — as you've probably noticed — a flaw in my logic. I claim to be a liar. Outright, without any guile, and straightforward.

Yet, after declaring myself to be a liar, I have proceeded to write a book about my life. So, therefore, how can you trust the story itself? If it's being told by a liar, won't it all be false? In fact, how can you trust that I'm a liar? If I always lie, then wouldn't I have had to be lying about saying that I'm a liar?

Now you see why I mentioned brain freezes, eh? Let me clarify. I *have been* a liar. Most of my life is a sham — the heroics I'm known for, the life I've led, the fame I've enjoyed. Those are the lies.

The things I'm telling you here are factual. In this case, I can only prove that I'm a liar by telling the truth, though I will also include some lies — which I will point out — to act as object lessons proving the truth that I'm a liar.

Got that?

I was thrown off the bedroll and rammed against the glass wall as the *Dragonaut* shook, twisting away from the explosion that was still visible in the darkness outside my wall. Our vessel didn't appear to have been damaged, but it had been a close call.

I rubbed my head, coming awake. Then cursed quietly and scrambled out the door. At that moment, the *Dragonaut* lurched again, moving to the right. I was thrown off my feet as a flaring missile just barely missed our ship. It trailed a glow of flaming smoke behind it, then exploded off in the distance.

I righted myself just in time to see something else shoot past the *Dragonaut* — not another missile, but something with roaring engines. It looked alarmingly like an F-15 fighter jet.

"Shattering Glass!" I exclaimed, forcing myself to my feet and pulling out my Oculator's Lenses. I shoved them on and rushed to the cockpit. I arrived, stumbling through the doorway as Bastille pointed. "Left!" she yelled. "Bank left!"

I could see sweat on Australia's face as she turned the *Dragonaut* to the side, out of the way of the approaching fighter. I barely managed to stay on my feet as the ship dodged another missile.

I groaned, shaking my head. Kaz stood on a seat, hands leaning against the control dash, looking out the other eyeball. "Now *this*," the short man proclaimed, "is more like it! It's been ages since anyone shot missiles at me!"

Bastille gave him a harsh stare, then glanced to the side as I rushed up, grabbing a chair to steady myself.

Ahead, the fighter launched another missile.

I focused, trying to get my Talent to engage at a distance and destroy the jet like it did guns. Nothing happened.

Australia twisted the *Dragonaut* just in time, throwing me to the side, my hands slipping free of the chair. That's one problem with making everything out of glass. Handholds become rather difficult to maintain.

Bastille managed to stay up, but she had on her Warrior's Lenses, which enhanced her physical abilities. Kaz didn't have any Lenses on, but he seemed to have an excellent sense of balance.

I rubbed my head as the missile exploded off in the distance. "This shouldn't be possible!" I said. "That jet has so many moving parts, my Talent should have been able to stop it easy."

Bastille shook her head, glancing at me. "Glass missiles, Alcatraz."

"I've never seen *anything* like this," Australia agreed, glancing over her shoulder, watching the jet's fire trails. "That ship isn't Hushlander technology — or, well, not completely. It's some kind of fusion. Parts of the jet body look like they're metal, but others look like they're glass."

Bastille gave me a hand to help me back up to my feet.

"Aw, birchnuts!" Kaz swore, pointing. I squinted, leaning against the chair, watching the jet bank and turn back toward us. It seemed more maneuverable, more precise, than a regular jet. As it turned toward us, its cockpit started to glow.

Not the whole cockpit. Just the glass covering it. I frowned, and my friends seemed equally confused.

The jet's glass canopy shot forth a beam of glowing white power, directed at us. It hit one of the dragon's wings, spraying out shards of ice and snow. The wing, caught in the grip of the cold, froze in place. Then, as its mechanisms tried to force it to move, the wing shattered into a thousand pieces.

"Frostbringer's Lens!" Bastille shouted as the *Dragonaut* rocked.

"That was no Lens!" Australia said. "That fired from the canopy glass!"

"Amazing!" Kaz said, holding on to his seat as the ship rocked.

We're going to die, I thought.

It wasn't the first time I'd felt that icy pit of terror, that sense of horrible doom that came from thinking I was going to die. I felt it on the altar when I was about to get sacrificed, I felt it when Blackburn shot me with his Torturer's Lens, and I felt it as I watched the F-15 turn back toward us for another run.

I never got used to that feeling. It's kind of like getting punched in the face by your own mortality.

And mortality has a wicked right hook.

"We need to do something!" I shouted as the *Dragonaut* lurched. Australia, however, had her eyes closed — I'd later learn that she was mentally compensating for the lost wing, keeping us in the air. Ahead of us, the fighter's cockpit began glowing again.

"We *are* doing something," Bastille said.

"What?"

"Stalling!"

"For what?"

Something thumped up above. I glanced up, apprehensive as I looked through the translucent glass. Bastille's mother, Draulin, stood up on the roof of the *Dragonaut*. A majestic cloak fluttered out behind her, and she wore her steel armor. She carried a Sword of Crystallia.

I'd seen one once before, during the Library infiltration. Bastille had pulled it out to fight against Alivened monsters. I'd thought, maybe, that I'd remembered the sword's ridiculous size wrong — that perhaps it had simply *looked* big next to Bastille.

I was wrong. The sword was enormous, at least five feet long from tip of blade to hilt. It glittered, made completely of the crystal from which the Crystin, and Crystallia itself, get their name.

(The knights aren't terribly original with names. Crystin, Crystallia, crystals. One time when I was allowed into Crystallia, I jokingly dubbed my potato a "Potatin potato, grown and crafted in the Fields of Potatallia." The knights were not amused. Maybe I should have used my carrot instead.)

Draulin stepped across the head of our flying dragon, her armored boots clinking against the glass. Somehow, she managed to retain a sure footing despite the wind and the shaking vehicle.

The jet fired a beam from its Frostbringer's glass, aiming for another wing. Bastille's mother jumped, leaping through the air, cloak flapping. She landed on the wing itself, raising her crystalline sword. The beam of frost hit the sword and disappeared in a puff. Bastille's mother barely even bent beneath the blow. She stood powerfully, her armored visor obscuring her face.

The cockpit fell silent. It seemed impossible to me that Draulin had managed such a feat. Yet, as I waited, the jet fired again, and once again Bastille's mother managed to get in front of the beam and destroy it.

"She's . . . standing on *top* of the *Dragonaut*," I said as I watched through the glass.

"Yes," Bastille said.

"We appear to be going several hundred miles an hour."

"About that."

"She's blocking laser beams fired by a jet airplane."

"Yes."

"Using nothing but her sword."

"She's a Knight of Crystallia," Bastille said, looking away. "That's the sort of thing they do."

I fell silent, watching Bastille's mother run the entire length of the *Dragonaut* in the space of a couple seconds, then block an ice beam fired at us from behind.

Kaz shook his head. "Those Crystin," he said. "They take the fun out of everything." He smiled toothily.

To this day, I haven't been able to tell if Kaz genuinely has a death wish, or if he just likes to act that way. Either way, he's a loon. But, then, he's a Smedry. That's virtually a synonym for "insane, foolhardy lunatic."

I glanced at Bastille. She watched her mother move above, and seemed longing, yet ashamed at the same time.

That's the sort of thing they expect her to be able to do, I thought. *That's why they took her knighthood from her — because they thought she wasn't up to their standards.*

"Um, trouble!" Australia said. She'd opened her eyes, but looked very frazzled as she sat with her hand on the glowing panel. Up ahead, the fighter jet was charging its glass again — and it had just released another missile.

"Grab on!" Bastille said, getting ahold of a chair. I did the same, for all the good it did. I was again tossed to the side as Australia dodged. Up above, Draulin managed to block the Frostbringer's ray, but it looked close.

The missile exploded just a short distance from the body of the *Dragonaut.*

We can't keep doing this, I thought. *Australia looks like she can barely hold on, and Bastille's mother will get tired eventually.*

We're in serious trouble.

I picked myself up, rubbing my arm, blinking away the afterimage of the missile explosion. I could feel something as the jet shot past us. A dark twisting in my stomach, just like the feeling I'd felt on the runway. It felt a little like the sense that told me when an Oculator nearby was using one of their Lenses. Yet, this was different. Tainted somehow.

The creature from the airport was in that jet. Before, it had shot the Lens out of my hand. Now it used a jet that could fire on me without exploding. Somehow, it seemed to understand how to use both Free Kingdoms technology and Hushlands technology together.

And that seemed a very, very dangerous combination.

"Do we have any weapons on board the ship?" I asked.

Bastille shrugged. "I have a dagger."

"That's it?"

"We've got you, cousin," Australia said. "You're an Oculator and a Smedry of the pure line. You're better than any regular weapons."

Great, I thought. I glanced up at Bastille's mother, who stood on the nose of the dragon. "How can she stand there like that?"

"Grappler's Glass," Bastille said. "It sticks to other kinds of glass, and she's got some plates of it on the bottom of her boots."

"Do we have any more?"

Bastille paused, then — without questioning me — she rushed over to a side of the cockpit, searching through a glass trunk on the floor. She came up a few moments later with a pair of boots.

"These will do the same thing," she said, handing them to me. They looked far too large for my feet.

The ship rocked as Australia dodged another missile. I didn't know how many of those the jet had, but it seemed like it could carry far more than it should be able to. I slumped back against the wall as the *Dragonaut* shook, then I pulled the first boot on over my own shoe and tied the laces tight.

"What are you doing?" Bastille asked. "You're not planning to go up there, are you?"

I pulled on the other boot. My heart was beginning to beat faster.

"What do you expect to do, Alcatraz?" Bastille asked quietly. "My mother is a full Knight of Crystallia. What help could you possibly be to her?"

I hesitated, and Bastille flushed slightly at how harsh the words had sounded, though it wasn't really in her nature to retract things like that. Besides, she was right.

What *was* I thinking?

Kaz moved over to us. "This is bad, Bastille."

"Oh, you finally noticed that, did you?" she snapped.

"Don't get touchy," he said. "I may like a good ride, but I hate sudden stops as much as the next Smedry. We need an escape plan."

Bastille fell silent for a moment. "How many of us can you use your Talent to transport?"

"Up here, in the sky?" he asked. "Without any place to flee? I'm not sure, honestly. I doubt I'd be able to get all of us."

"Take Alcatraz," Bastille said. "Go now."

My stomach twisted. "No," I said, standing. My feet immediately locked on to the glass floor of the cockpit. When I tried to take a step, however, my foot came free. When I put it down again, it locked into place.

Nice, I thought, trying not to focus on what I was about to do.

"Chestnuts, kid!" Kaz swore. "You might not be the brightest torch in the row, but I don't want to see you get killed. I owe your father that much. Come with me — we'll get lost, then head to Nalhalla."

"And leave the others to die?"

"We'll be just fine," Bastille said quickly. Too quickly.

The thing is, I paused. It may not seem very heroic, but a large part of me wanted to go with Kaz. My hands were sweating, my heart thumping. The ship rocked as another missile nearly hit us. I saw a spiderweb of cracks appear on the right side of the cockpit.

I could run. Escape. Nobody would blame me. I wanted so badly to do just that.

I didn't. This might look like bravery, but I assure you that I'm a coward at heart. I'll prove that at another time. For now, simply believe that it wasn't bravery that spurred me on, it was pride.

I was the Oculator. Australia had said I was their main weapon. I determined to see what I could do. "I'm going up," I said. "How do I get there?"

"Hatch on the ceiling," Bastille finally said. "In the same room where you came up on the rope. Come on, I'll show you."

Kaz caught her arm as she moved. "Bastille, you're actually going to let him do this?"

She shrugged. "If he wants to get himself killed, what business is it of mine? It just means one less person we have to worry about saving."

I smiled wanly. I knew Bastille well enough to hear the concern in her voice. She was actually worried about me. Or, perhaps, just angry at me. With her, the difference is difficult to judge.

She took off down the corridor, and I followed, quickly getting the rhythm of walking with the boots. As soon as they touched glass, they locked on, making me stable — something I appreciated when the ship rocked from another blast. I moved a little more slowly than normal in them, but they were worth it.

I caught up to Bastille in the room, and she threw a lever, opening a hatch in the ceiling.

"Why *are* you letting me do this?" I asked. "Usually you complain when I try to get myself killed."

"Yeah, well, at least this time *I* won't be the one who looks bad if you die. My mother's the knight in charge of protecting you."

I raised an eyebrow.

"Plus," she said. "Maybe you'll be able to do something. Who knows. You've gotten lucky in the past."

I smiled, and somehow the vote of confidence — such that it was — bolstered me. I glanced up. "How do I get out there?"

"Your feet stick to the walls, stupid."

"Oh, right," I said. Taking a deep breath, I stepped up onto the side of the wall. It was easier than I'd thought it would be — silimatic technicians say that Grappler's Glass works to hold your entire body in place, not just your feet. Either way, I found it rather easy (if a little disorienting) to walk up the side of the wall and out onto the top of the *Dragonaut*.

Let's talk about air. You see, air is a really nifty thing. It lets us make cool sounds with our mouths, it carries smells from one person to another, and without it nobody would be able to play air guitar. Oh, and there is that other thing it does: It lets us breathe, allowing all animal life to exist on the planet. Great stuff, air.

The thing about air is, you don't really think about it until (a) you don't have enough or (b) you have *way* too much of it. That second one is particularly nasty when you get hit in the face by a bunch of it going somewhere in the neighborhood of three hundred miles an hour.

The wind buffeted me backward, and only the Grappler's Glass on my feet kept me upright. Even with it, I bent backward precariously, like some gravity-defying dancer in a music video. I'd have felt kind of cool about that if I hadn't been terrified for my life.

Bastille must have seen my predicament, for she rushed toward the cockpit. I'm still not sure how she persuaded Australia to slow the ship — by all accounts, that should have been a very stupid thing to do. Still, the wind lessened to a slightly manageable speed, and I was able to clomp my way across the top of the ship toward Draulin.

Massive wings beat beside me, and the dragon's snake body rolled. Each step was sure, though. I passed beneath stars and moon, the cloud cover glowing beneath us. I arrived near the front of the vehicle just as Draulin blocked another blast of Frostbringer's ray. As I grew closer, she spun toward me.

"Lord *Smedry*?" she asked, voice muffled by both wind and her helmet. "What in the name of the first sands are you doing here?"

"I've come to help!" I yelled above the howl of wind.

She seemed dumbfounded. The jet shot past in the night sky, rounding for another attack.

"Go back!" she said, waving with an armored hand.

"I'm an Oculator," I said, pointing to my Lenses. "I can stop the Frostbringer's ray."

It was true. An Oculator can use his Oculator's Lenses to counter an enemy's attack. I'd seen my grandfather do it when dueling Blackburn. I'd never tried it myself, but, I figured it couldn't be that hard.

I was completely wrong, of course. It happens to the best of us at times.

Draulin cursed, running across the dragon's back to block another blast. The ship rolled, nearly making me sick, and I was suddenly struck by just how high up I was. I crouched down, holding my stomach, waiting for the world to orient itself again. When it did, Draulin was standing beside me.

"Go back down!" she yelled. "You can be of no help here!"

"I —"

"Idiot!" she yelled. "You're going to get us killed!"

I fell silent, the wind tussling my hair. I felt shocked to be treated so, but it was probably no more than I deserved. I turned away, clomping back toward the hatch, embarrassed.

To the side, the jet fired a missile. The glass on its cockpit fired another Frostbringer's ray.

And the *Dragonaut* didn't dodge.

I spun toward the cockpit and could just barely see Australia slumped over her control panel, dazed. Bastille was trying to slap her awake — she's particularly good at anything that requires slapping — and Kaz was furiously trying to make the ship respond.

We lurched, but the wrong way. Draulin cried out, barely slicing her sword through the icy beam as she stumbled. She vaporized it, but the missile continued on, directly toward us.

Directly toward me.

I've talked about the uneasy truce my Talent and I have. Neither of us is really ever in control. I can usually break things if I really want to, but rarely in exactly the way I want. And, my Talent often breaks things when I don't want it to.

What I lack in control, I make up for in power. I watched that missile coming, saw its glass length reflect the starlight, and saw the trail of smoke leading back to the fighter behind.

I stared at my reflection in oncoming death. Then, I raised my hand and released my Talent.

The missile shattered, shards of glass spraying from it, twinkling and spinning into the midnight air. Then, those shards exploded, vaporizing to powdered dust, which sprayed around me, missing me by several inches on each side.

The smoke from the missile's engine was still blowing forward, and it licked my fingers. Immediately, the line of smoke quivered. I screamed and a wave of power shot from my chest, pulsing up the line of smoke like water in a tube, moving toward the fighter, which was screaming along in the same path its missile had taken.

The wave of power hit the jet. All was silent for a moment.

Then, the fighter just . . . fell apart. It didn't explode, like one might see in an action movie. Its separate pieces simply departed one from another. Screws fell out, panels of metal were thrown free, pieces of glass separated from wing and cockpit. In seconds, the entire machine looked like a box of spare parts that had been carelessly tossed into the air.

The mess shot over the top of the *Dragonaut,* then fell toward the clouds below. As the pieces disbursed, I caught a glimpse of an angry face in the midst of the metal. It was the pilot, twisting among the discarded parts. In an oddly surreal moment, his eyes met mine, and I saw cold hatred in them.

The face was not all human. Half looked normal, the other half was an amalgamation of screws, springs, nuts, and bolts — not unlike the pieces of the jet falling around it. One of his eyes was of the deepest, blackest glass.

He disappeared into the darkness.

I gasped suddenly, feeling incredibly weak. Bastille's mother crouched, one hand steadying herself against the roof, watching me with an expression I couldn't see through her knightly faceplate.

Only then did I notice the cracks in the top of the *Dragonaut.* They spread out from me in a spiral pattern, as if my feet had been the source of some great impact.

Looking desperately, I saw that most of the giant flying dragon now bore flaws or cracks of some kind.

My Talent — unpredictable as always — had shattered the glass beneath me as I'd used it to destroy the jet. Slowly, terribly, the massive dragon began to droop. Another of the wings fell free, the glass cracking and breaking. The *Dragonaut* lurched.

I'd saved the ship . . . but I'd also destroyed it.

We began to plummet downward.

CHAPTER 5

Now, there are several things you should consider doing if you are plummeting to your death atop a glass dragon in the middle of the ocean. Those things do *not,* mind you, include getting into an extended discussion of classical philosophy.

Leave that to professionals like me.

I want you to think about a ship. No, not a flying dragon ship like the one that was falling apart beneath me as I fell to my death. Focus. I obviously survived the crash, since this book is written in the first person.

I want you to think of a regular ship. The wooden kind, meant for sailing on the ocean. A ship owned by a man named Theseus, a Greek king immortalized by the writer Plutarch.

Plutarch was a silly little Greek historian best known for being born about three centuries too late, for having a great fascination with dead people, and for being *way* too long-winded. (He produced well over eight-hundred-thousand words' worth of writing. The Honorable Council of Fantasy Writers Whose Books Are Way Too Long — good old THCoFWWBAWTL — is considering making him an honorary member.)

Plutarch wrote a metaphor about the Ship of Theseus. You see, once the great king Theseus died, the people wanted to remember him. They decided to preserve his ship for future generations.

The ship got old, and its planks — as wood obstinately insists on doing — began to rot. So, the people replaced the rotting planks. After that, other pieces got old, and they replaced those too.

This continued for years. Eventually, every single part on the ship had been replaced. So, Plutarch relates an argument that many philosophers wonder about. Is the ship still the Ship of Theseus? People call it that. Everyone knows it is. Yet, there's a problem. None of the pieces are actually from the ship that Theseus used.

Is it the same ship?

I think it isn't. That ship is gone, buried, rotted. The copy everyone then *called* the Ship of Theseus was really just a . . . copy. It might have looked the same, but looks can be deceiving.

Now, what does this have to do with my story? Everything. You see, I'm that ship. Don't worry. I'll probably explain it to you eventually.

The *Dragonaut* fell into the clouds. The puffs of white passed around me in a furious maelstrom. Then, we were out of them, and I could see something very dark and very vast beneath me.

The ocean. I had that same feeling as before — the terrible thought that we were all going to die. And this time, it was my fault.

Stupid mortality.

The *Dragonaut* lurched, taking my stomach along with it. The mighty wings continued to beat, reflecting diffuse starlight that shone through the clouds. I twisted, looking to the cockpit, and saw Kaz concentrating, hand on the panel. Sweat beaded on his brow, but he managed to keep the ship in the air.

Something cracked. I looked down, realizing that I was standing in the very center of the broken portion of glass.

Uh-oh . . .

The glass beneath me shattered, but fortunately the ship

twisted at that moment, lurching upward. I was thrown down into the body of the vessel. I hit the glass floor, then had the peace of mind to slam one of my feet against the wall — locking it into place — as the ship writhed.

Kaz was doing an impressive job. The four remaining wings beat furiously, and the ship wasn't falling as quickly. We'd gone from a plummet of doom into a controlled spiral of doom.

I twisted, standing, the Grappler's Glass giving me enough stability to walk back to the cockpit. As I walked, I took off my Lenses and tucked them into their pocket, feeling lucky that I hadn't lost them in the chaos.

Inside, I found Bastille huddled over Australia, who looked very groggy. My cousin was bleeding from a blow to the head — I later learned she'd been thrown sideways into the wall when the ship began to fall.

I knew exactly what that felt like.

Bastille managed to strap poor Australia into a harness of some kind. Kaz was still focused on keeping us in the air. "Blasted thing," he said through gritted teeth, "why do you tall people have to fly up so high?"

I could just barely see land approaching ahead of us, and I felt a thrill of hope. At that moment, the back half of the dragon broke off, taking two more of the wings with it. We staggered in the air again, spinning, and the wall beside me exploded outward from the pressure.

Australia screamed, Kaz swore. I fell down on my back, knees bent, feet still planted on the floor.

And Bastille was sucked out the opening in the wall.

Now, I'll tell you time and time again that I'm not a hero. However, sometimes I *am* a bit quick-witted. As I saw Bastille shoot past me, I knew that I wouldn't be able to grab her in time.

I couldn't grab her, but I *could* kick her. So I did.

I slammed my foot into her side as she passed by, as if to shove her out the hole. Fortunately, she stuck to my foot — for, if you will remember, she was wearing a jacket made with glass fibers.

Bastille whipped out of the *Dragonaut,* her jacket stuck to the Grappler's Glass on the bottom of my foot. She twisted about, surprised, but grabbed my ankle to steady herself. This, of course, pulled me up and toward her — though fortunately my other foot was still planted on the glass floor.

Bastille held on to one foot, as the other stuck to the ship. It was not a pleasant sensation.

I yelled in pain as Kaz managed to angle the broken machine toward the beach. We crashed into the sand — even more glass breaking — and everything became a jumbled mess of bodies and debris.

★

I blinked awake, regaining consciousness a few minutes after the crash. I found myself lying on my back, staring out the broken hole of the ceiling. There was an open patch in the clouds, and I could see the stars.

"Uh . . . ," a voice said. "Is everyone okay?"

I twisted about, brushing bits of glass from my face — fortunately, the cockpit appeared to be made out of something like Free Kingdoms safety glass. Though it had shattered into shards, the pieces were surprisingly dull, and I hadn't been cut at all.

Australia — the one who had spoken — sat, holding her head where it was still bleeding. She looked about, seeming dazed. The pathetic remains of the *Dragonaut* lay broken around us, like the long-dead carcass of some mythical beast. The eyes had both shattered, and I sat in the skull. One of the wings jutted up a short distance away, pointing into the air.

Bastille groaned beside me, her jacket now laced with a spiderweb of lines. It had absorbed some of the shock from the landing for her. My legs, unfortunately, didn't have any such glass, and they ached from being yanked about.

There was a rustling a short distance away, up where the beach turned into trees. Suddenly, Kaz walked out of the forest, looking completely unbruised and unhurt.

"Well!" he said, surveying the beach. "That was certainly interesting. Anybody dead? Raise your hand if you are."

"What if you *feel* like you're dead?" Bastille asked, pulling herself free from her jacket.

"Raise a finger, then," Kaz said, walking down the beach toward us.

I won't say which one she raised.

"Wait," I said, wobbling a bit as I stood. "You got thrown all that way, but you're all right?"

"Of course I didn't get thrown that far," Kaz said with a laugh. "I got lost right about the time when we crashed, and I just found my way back. Sorry I missed the impact — but it didn't look like a whole lot of fun."

Smedry Talents. I shook my head, checking my pockets to make certain my Lenses had survived. Fortunately, the padding had protected them. But, as I worked, I realized something. "Bastille! Your mother!"

Just then, a sheet of glass rattled and was shoved over by something beneath it. Draulin stood up, and I heard a faint moan from inside her helmet. In one hand, she still held her Crystin blade. She reached up, sheathing it into a strap on her back, then pulled the helmet off. A pile of sweaty, silver hair fell around her face. She turned to regard the wreckage.

I was a little surprised to see her in such good shape. Of course, I should have realized that the armor she wore was of silimatic technology. It had worked as an even better cushion than Bastille's jacket.

"Where *are* we?" Bastille asked, picking her way across a field of broken glass, now wearing only a black T-shirt tucked into her militaristic trousers.

It was a good question. The forest looked vaguely junglelike. Waves quietly rolled up and down the starlit beach, grabbing bits of glass and towing them into the ocean.

"Egypt, I guess," Australia said. She held a bandage to her head, but otherwise seemed to have come out all right. "I mean, that's where we were heading, right? We were almost there when we crashed."

"No," Draulin said, stalking across the beach toward us. "Lord Kazan was required to take over control of the ship when you lost consciousness, which means . . ."

"My Talent came into play," Kaz said. "In other words, we're lost."

"Not *that* lost," Bastille said. "Isn't that the Worldspire?"

She pointed out across the ocean. And, just vaguely in the distance, I could see what appeared to be a tower rising from the ocean. Considering the distance, it must have been enormous.

I was later to learn that enormous was a severe underestimate. The Worldspire is said by the Free Kingdomers to be the exact center of the world. It's a massive glass spike running from the upper atmosphere directly into the center of the planet — which is, of course, made of glass. Isn't everything?

"You're right," Draulin said. "That means we're probably somewhere in the Kalmarian Wilds. Well outside the Hushlands."

"Well, that shouldn't be a problem," Kaz said.

"You think you can get us to Nalhalla, my lord?" Draulin asked.

"Probably."

I turned. "What about the Library of Alexandria?"

"You still want to go *there*?" Draulin asked.

"Of course."

"I don't know if —"

"Draulin," I said, "don't make me force you to hop on one foot again."

She fell silent.

"I agree with Alcatraz," Kaz said, walking over to pick through the rubble. "If my father's in Alexandria, then he's undoubtedly getting into trouble. If he's in trouble, that means I'm missing out on some serious fun. Now, let's see if we can salvage anything. . . ."

I watched him work, and soon Draulin joined him, picking through the pieces. Bastille walked up beside me.

"Thanks," she said. "For saving me when I fell out of the side of the dragon, I mean."

"Sure. I'll kick you any time you want."

She snorted softly. "You're a real friend."

I smiled. Considering that we'd crashed so soundly, it was remarkable that nobody had been severely hurt. Actually, you may find this annoying. It would have been a better story if someone had died here. An early fatality can really make a book seem much more tense, as it lets people realize how dangerous things can be.

You have to remember, however, that this is not fiction, but a real-life account. I can't help it if all of my friends were too selfish to do the narratively proper thing and get themselves killed off to hike up the tension of my memoirs.

I've spoken to them at length about this. If it makes you feel better, Bastille dies by the end of this book.

Oh, you didn't want to hear that? I'm sorry. You'll just have to forget that I wrote it. There are several convenient ways to do that. I hear hitting yourself on the head with a blunt object can be very effective. You should try using one of Brandon Sanderson's fantasy novels. They're big enough, and goodness knows, that's really the only useful thing to do with them.

Bastille — completely unaware that she was condemned — glanced at the half-buried dragon's head. Its broken eyes stared out toward the jungle, its maw opened slightly, teeth cracked. "It seems such a sad end for the *Dragonaut*," she said. "So much powerful glass wasted."

"Is there any way to . . . I don't know, fix it?"

She shrugged. "The silimatic engine is gone, and that's

what gave the glass its power. I supposed if you could get a new engine, it would still work. But, cracked as the ship is, it would probably make more sense to smelt the whole thing down."

The others came up with a couple of backpacks full of food and supplies. Kaz eventually let out a whoop of joy, then dug out a little bowler of a hat, which he put on. This was joined by a vest he wore under his jacket. It was an odd combination, since the jacket itself — along with his trousers — were made of heavyweight, rugged material. He came across looking like some cross between Indiana Jones and a British gentleman.

"We ready?" he asked.

"Almost," I said, finally pulling off the boots with the Grappler's Glass on them. "Any way to turn these off?" I held up the boot, critically eyeing the bottom, which was now stuck with shards of glass and — not surprisingly — sand.

"For most people there is no way," Draulin said, sitting down on a piece of the wreckage, then taking off her armored boots. She pulled out a few pieces of specially shaped glass and slid them into place. "We simply cover them with plates like these, so the boots stick to those instead."

I nodded. The plates in question had soles and heels on the bottom, and probably felt just like regular shoes.

"You, however, are an Oculator," she said.

"What does that have to do with it?"

"Oculators aren't like regular people, Alcatraz," Australia said, smiling. Her head had stopped bleeding, and she'd tied a bandage to it. A pink one. I had no idea where she had found it.

"Indeed, my lord," Draulin said. "You can use Lenses, but you also have some limited power over silimatic glass, what we call 'technology.'"

"You mean, like the engine?" I asked, slipping on my Oculator's Lenses.

Draulin nodded. "Try deactivating the boots like you would Lenses."

I did so, touching them. Surprisingly, the sand and glass dropped free, the boots becoming inert.

"Those boots had been given a silimatic charge," Australia explained. "Kind of like batteries you use in the Hushlands. The boots will run out eventually. Until then, an Oculator can turn them off and on."

"One of the great mysteries of our age," Draulin said, her boots replaced. The way she said it indicated that she didn't really care how or why things worked, only that they did.

Me, I was more curious. I'd been told several times about Free Kingdomer technology. It seemed a simple distinction to me. Magic was that sort of thing that only worked for certain people, while technology — often called silimatics — worked for anyone. Australia had been able to fly the *Dragonaut,* but so had Kaz. It was technology.

But what I had just learned seemed to indicate that there was a relationship between this technology of theirs and Oculatory powers. However, the conversation reminded me of something else. I didn't have any idea if we were closer to Alexandria now than we had been before, but it seemed a good idea to try contacting my grandfather again.

I slipped on the Courier's Lenses and concentrated. Unfortunately, I wasn't able to get anything out of them. I left them on just in case, then stuffed the Grappler's Glass boots into one of the packs.

I slung it over my shoulder; however, Bastille took it from me. I shot her a frown.

"Sorry," she said. "My mother's orders."

"You don't need to carry anything, Lord Smedry," Draulin said, hefting another pack. "Let Squire Bastille do it."

"I can carry my own backpack, Draulin," I snapped.

"Oh?" she asked. "And if we get attacked, do you not need to be ready and agile so that you can use your Lenses to defend us?" She turned away from me. "Squire Bastille is good at carrying things. Allow her to do this — it will let her be useful and make her feel a sense of accomplishment."

Bastille flushed. I opened my mouth to argue some more, but Bastille shot me a glance that quieted me.

Fine, I thought. We all looked toward Kaz, ready to go. "Onward, then!" the short man said, taking off across the sand up toward the trees.

CHAPTER 6

Adults are not idiots.

Often, in books such as this one, the opposite impression is given. Adults in those stories will either (a) get captured, (b) disappear conspicuously when there is trouble, or (c) refuse to help.

(I'm not sure what authors have against adults, but everyone seems to hate them to an extent usually reserved for dogs and mothers. Why else make them out to be such idiots? "Ah, look, the dark lord of evil has come to attack the castle! Annnnd, there's my lunch break. Have fun saving the world on your own, kids!")

In the real world, adults tend to get involved in everything, whether you want them to or not. They won't disappear when the dark lord appears, though they may try to sue him. This discrepancy is yet another proof that most books are fantasies while this book is utterly true and invaluable. You see, in this book, I will make it completely clear that all adults are *not* idiots.

They are, however, hairy.

Adults are like hairy kids who like to tell others what to do. Despite what other books may claim, they do have their uses. They can reach things on high shelves, for instance. (Though, Kaz would argue that such high shelves shouldn't be necessary. Reference Reason number sixty-three, which will be explained at a later point.)

Regardless, I often wish that the two groups — adults and kids — could find a way to get along better. Some sort of treaty or something. The biggest problem is, the adults have one of the most effective recruitment strategies in the world.

Give them enough time, and they'll turn *any* kid into one of them.

We entered the jungle.

"Everyone remember to *stay in sight* of someone else in the group," Kaz said. "There's no telling where we'll leave you if you get separated!"

With that, Kaz pulled out a machete and began to cut his way through the undergrowth. I glanced back at the beach, bidding silent farewell to the translucent dragon, cracked from the landing, its body slowly being buried in sand from the rising tide. One wing still hung up in the air, as if in defiance of its death.

"You were the most majestic thing I'd ever seen," I whispered. "Rest well." A little melodramatic, true, but it felt appropriate. Then I quickly rushed after the others, careful not to lose sight of Draulin, who walked in the rear.

The jungle was thick, and the canopy overhead made the darkness near absolute. Draulin pulled an antiquated-looking lantern from her pack, then tapped it with one finger. It started to glow, the flame coming to life without needing a match. Even with it, however, it felt creepy to be traveling through a dense jungle in the middle of the night.

In order to still my nerves, I moved to walk by Bastille. She, however, didn't want to talk. I eventually worked my way up through the column until I was behind Kaz. I figured that he and I had started off on the wrong foot, and I hoped I could patch things up a bit.

Those of you who recall the events of the first book will realize that this was quite a change in me. For most of my life, I'd been abandoned by family after family. It was tough to blame them, however, since I'd spent my childhood breaking everything in sight. I'd gone on such a rampage that I would have made the proverbial bull in the proverbial china shop look unproverbially good by proverbial comparison. (Personally, I don't even know how he'd fit through the door. Proverbially.)

Regardless, I had grown into the habit of pushing people away as soon as I got to know them — abandoning them before they could abandon me. It had been tough to realize what I was doing, but I was already starting to change.

Kaz was my uncle. My father's brother. For a kid who had spent most of his life thinking that he had no living relatives, having Kaz think I was a fool was a big deal. I wanted desperately to show him that I was capable.

Kaz glanced at me as he chopped at the foliage — though he only tended to cut away things up to his own height of four feet, leaving the rest of us to get branches in our faces. "Well?" he asked.

"I wanted to apologize for that whole midget thing."

He shrugged.

"It's just that . . . ," I said. "Well, I figured with all of the magic and stuff they have in the Free Kingdoms, they would have been able to cure dwarfism by now."

"They haven't been able to cure stupidity, either," he said. "So I guess we won't be able to help you."

I blushed. "I . . . didn't mean . . ."

Kaz chuckled, slicing off a couple of fronds. "Look, it's all right. I'm used to this. I just want you to understand that I don't need to be *cured*."

"But . . . ," I said, trying hard to express what I felt without being offensive, "isn't being short like you a genetic disease?"

"Genetic, yes," Kaz said. "But is it disease just because it's different? I mean, you're an Oculator; that's genetic too. Would *you* like to be cured?"

"That's different," I said.

"Is it?"

I paused to think about it. "I don't know," I finally said. "But don't you get tired of being short?"

"Don't you get tired of being tall?"

"I . . ." It was tough to come up with an answer to that one. I really wasn't all that tall — barely five feet, now that I'd launched into my teens. Still, I was tall compared with him.

"Now, personally," Kaz continued, "I think you tall people are really missing out. Why, the entire world would be a better place if you were all shorter."

I raised an eyebrow.

"You look doubtful," Kaz said, smiling. "Obviously you need to be introduced to The List!"

"The List?"

From behind, I heard Australia sigh. "Don't encourage him, Alcatraz."

"Hush, you!" Kaz said, eyeing Australia and eliciting a bit of an *eep* from her. "The List is a time-tested and scientifically researched collection of facts that *prove* that short people are better off than tall ones."

He glanced at me. "Confused?"

I nodded.

"Slowness of thought," he said. "A common ailment of tall people. Reason number forty-seven: Tall people's heads are in a thinner atmosphere than those of short people, so the tall people get less oxygen. That makes it so that their brains don't work quite as well."

With that, he chopped his way through the edge of the forest and walked out into a clearing. I stopped in the path, then glanced at Australia.

"We're not sure if he's serious or not," she whispered. "But, he really *does* keep that List of his."

After getting a glare from Bastille for pausing for so

long, I rushed out into the clearing with Kaz. I was surprised to see that the jungle broke just a little farther out, giving us a view of . . .

"Paris?" I asked in shock. "That's the Eiffel Tower!"

"Ah, is that what that is?" Kaz asked, scribbling something on a notepad. "Great! We're back in the Hushlands. Not as badly lost as I thought."

"But . . . ," I said. "We were on another continent! How did we cross the ocean?"

"We're lost, kid," Kaz said, as if that explained everything. "Anyway, I'll get us where we need to be. Always trust the short person to know his way! Reason number twenty-eight: Short people can find things easier and follow trails better because they're closer to the ground."

I stood, nearly dumbfounded. "But . . . there aren't any jungles near Paris!"

"He gets lost," Bastille said, walking up to me, "in some very incredible ways."

"I think this is the strangest Talent I've ever seen," I said. "And that's saying a lot."

She shrugged. "Didn't yours break a chicken once?"

"Good point."

Kaz led us back to the trees, cutting us a half pathway.

"So, your Talent can take you anywhere!" I said to the short man.

He shrugged. "Why do you think I was on the *Dragonaut*? In case things went wrong, I was to get you and your grandfather out of the Hushlands."

"Why even send the ship, then? You could have come got me on your own!"

He snorted. "I have to know what to look for, Al. I have to have a destination. Australia had to come so that we could use Lenses to contact you, and we figured it was a good idea to bring a Knight of Crystallia for protection. Besides, my Talent can be a little . . . unpredictable."

"I think they all can," I said.

He chuckled. "Well, that's the truth. Just hope you never have to see Australia after she's just gotten up in the morning. Anyway, we figured that rather than taking a chance on my Talent — which has occasionally gotten me lost for weeks — we should bring the ship."

"So . . . wait," I said. "We could be walking like this for weeks?"

"Maybe," Kaz said, parting some fronds, looking out. I peeked through beside him. What looked like a desert was sprawling out beyond us. He rubbed his chin in thought.

"Walnuts," he swore. "We're a bit off track." He let the fronds fall back into place and we continued walking.

Several weeks. My grandfather could be in danger. In fact, knowing Grandpa Smedry, he most definitely *was* in danger. Yet, I couldn't get to him because I was traipsing through the jungle, occasionally peering out through another clearing at . . .

"Dodger Stadium?" I asked. "I *know* there aren't any jungles there!"

"Must be up past the nosebleed seats," Kaz said, taking another turn, leading us in a different direction. It was already growing light, and dawn would soon arrive. As we started again, Draulin marched up beside me. "Lord Alcatraz? Might I have a moment of your time?"

I nodded slowly. Being called "lord" was still a little unsettling to me. What was required of me? Was I expected to sip tea and behead people? (If so, I certainly hoped I wouldn't need to do both at the same time.)

What did it mean to be called "lord"? I'll assume you've never had the honor, since I doubt any of you happen to be British royalty. (And, if by chance you are, then let me say, "Hello, Your Majesty! Welcome to my stupid book. Can I borrow some cash?")

It seemed that the Free Kingdomers had unrealistic expectations of me. I wasn't normally the type to doubt myself, but I'd rarely had a chance to be a leader. The more others started to look to me, the more I began to worry. What if I failed them?

"My lord," Draulin said. "I feel the need to apologize. I spoke quite out of turn to you while we were fighting atop the *Dragonaut*."

"It's all right," I said, shaking myself out of my moment of self-doubt. "We were in a tense situation."

"No, there is no excuse."

"Really," I said. "Anyone could have gotten snappish in a predicament like that."

"My lord," she said sternly, "a Knight of Crystallia isn't just 'anyone.' More is expected of us — not just in action, but in attitude as well. We don't just respect men of your station, we respect and serve all people. We must *always* strive to be the best, for the reputation of the entire order depends on it."

Bastille was walking just behind us. For some reason, I got the feeling that Draulin was preaching less to me, and more to her daughter. It seemed backhanded.

"Please," Draulin continued. "I would be more at peace if you would chastise me."

"Uh . . . okay," I said. (How does one scold a Knight of Crystallia some twenty years your senior? "Bad knight"? "Go straight to bed without polishing your sword"?)

"Consider yourself chastised," I said instead.

"Thank you."

"Aha!" Kaz called.

The line paused. Sunlight was beginning to peek through the canopy of leaves. Ahead, Kaz was looking out through some bushes. He flashed us a smile, then cut the bushes away with a swipe of the machete.

"I knew I'd find my way!" he said, gesturing out. I looked for the first time at the great Library of Alexandria — a place so entrenched in lore and mythology that I'd been taught about it even in Hushlander schools. One of the most dangerous buildings on the planet.

It was a one-room hut.

CHAPTER 7

I am a fish.

No, really. I am. I have fins, a tail, scales. I swim about, doing fishy things. This isn't a metaphor or a joke, but a real and honest fact. I am a fish.

More on this later.

"We came all this way for *that*?" I asked, looking at the hut. It stood on an open plain of sandy, scrubby ground. The roof looked like it was about to fall in.

"Yup, that's it," Kaz said, walking out of the jungle and down the slope toward the hut.

I glanced back at Bastille, who just shrugged. "I've never been here before."

"I have," Bastille's mother said. "Yes, that is the Library of Alexandria." She clomped out of the jungle. I shrugged, then followed her, Australia and Bastille joining me. As we walked, I glanced back at the jungle.

It, of course, had vanished. I stopped, but then thought better of asking. After everything that I'd been through in the last few months, a disappearing jungle wasn't really even all that odd.

I hurried to catch up to Kaz. "You're *sure* this is the place? I kind of expected it to look . . . well, a little less like a hut."

"You would have preferred a yurt?" Kaz asked, walking up to the doorway and peeking in. I followed.

Inside, a large set of stairs was cut into the ground. They led down into the depths of the earth. The dark opening seemed unnaturally black to me — like someone had cut a square in the floor and pulled away the fabric of existence with it.

"The Library," I said. "It's underground?"

"Of course," Kaz said. "What did you expect? This is the Hushlands — things like the Library of Alexandria need to keep a low profile."

Draulin walked up beside us, then pointed for Bastille to check the perimeter. She moved off. Draulin went the other way, scouting the area for danger.

"The Curators of Alexandria aren't like Librarians you've seen before, Al," Kaz said.

"What do you mean?"

"Well, they're undead wraiths, for one thing," he said, "though it's not really nice to be prejudiced against people because of their race."

I raised an eyebrow.

"Just saying . . . ," he said with a shrug. "Anyway, the Curators are older than the Librarians of Biblioden. Actually, the Curators are older than most things in this world. The Library of Alexandria was started back during the days of classical Greece. Alexandria was, after all, founded by Alexander the Great."

"Wait," I said. "He was a real person?"

"Of course he was," Australia said, joining us. "Why wouldn't he be?"

I shrugged. "I don't know. I guess I figured that all the things I'd learned in school were Librarian lies."

"Not all of them," Kaz said. "The Librarian teachings only *really* start to deviate from the truth about five hundred years back — about the time that Biblioden lived." He paused, scratching his face. "Of course, I guess they *do* lie about this place. I think they teach that it was destroyed."

I nodded. "By the Romans or something."

"Complete fabrication," Kaz said. "The Library outgrew its old location, so the Curators moved it here. Guess they wanted a place where they could hollow out as much ground as they wanted. It's kind of tough to find room inside a big city to store every book ever written."

"*Every* book?"

"Of course," Kaz said. "That's the point of this place. It's a storage of all knowledge ever recorded."

Suddenly, things started to make sense. "That's why my father came here and why Grandpa Smedry followed! Don't you see! My father can read texts in the Forgotten Language now; he has a set of Translator's Lenses like mine, forged from the Sands of Rashid."

"Yes," Kaz said. "And?"

"And so he came here," I said, looking at the stairway leading into the darkness. "He came for knowledge. Books in the Forgotten Language. He could study them here, learn what the ancient people — the Incarna — knew."

Australia and Kaz shared a glance.

"That's . . . not really all that likely, Alcatraz," Australia said.

"Why not?"

"The Curators gather the knowledge," Kaz said, "but they're not that great at sharing. They'll let you read a book, but they charge a terrible cost."

I felt a chill. "What cost?"

"Your soul," Australia said. "You can read one book, then you become one of them, to serve in the Library for eternity."

Great, I thought, glancing at Kaz. The shorter man looked troubled. "What?" I asked.

"I know your father, Al. We grew up together — he's my brother."

"And?"

"He's a true Smedry. Just like your grandfather. We don't tend to think things through. Things like charging into danger, like infiltrating Libraries, or . . ."

"Like reading a book that will cost you your soul?"

Kaz looked away. "I don't *think* he'd be that stupid. He'd get the knowledge he wanted, but he'd never be able to share it or use it. Even Attica wouldn't get *that* hungry for answers."

The comment begged another question. *If he didn't come for a book, then why visit?* I thought.

Draulin and Bastille arrived a few moments later. Now, you might have noticed something important. Look up the name Draulin on your favorite search engine. You won't get many results, and the ones you do get will probably be typos, not prisons. (Though, the two are related in that they are both things I tend to be affiliated with far too often.) Either way, there's no prison named Draulin, though there is one named Bastille.

(That last bit about the names — that is foreshadowing. So don't say I never give you anything.)

"Perimeter is secure," Draulin said. "No guards."

"There never are," Kaz said, glancing back at the stairs. "I've been here half a dozen times — mostly due to getting lost — though I've never gone in. The Curators don't guard the place. They don't need to — anyone who tries to steal even a single book will automatically lose their soul, whether they know about the rules or not."

I shivered.

"We should camp here," Draulin said, glancing over at the rising sun. "Most of us didn't get any sleep last night, and we shouldn't go down into the Library without our wits about us."

"Probably a good idea," Kaz said, yawning. "Plus, we don't really know if we *need* to go in. Al, you said my father visited this place. Did he go in?"

"I don't know," I said. "I couldn't tell for certain."

"Try the Lenses again," Australia said, nodding encouragingly — something that appeared to be one of her favorite gestures.

I was still wearing the Courier's Lenses; as before, I tried to contact my grandfather. All I received was a low buzz and a kind of wavering fuzz in my vision. "I'm trying," I said. "All I get is a blurry fuzz. Anyone know what that means?"

I glanced at Australia. She shrugged — for an Oculator, she sure didn't seem to know much. Then, I was one too, and I knew even less, so it was a little hard to judge.

"Don't ask me," Kaz said. "That ability skipped me, fortunately."

I looked over at Bastille.

"Don't look at her," Draulin said. "Bastille is a squire of Crystallia, not an Oculator."

I caught Bastille's eyes. She glanced at her mother.

"I command her to speak," I said.

"It means there's interference of some sort," Bastille said quickly. "Courier's Lenses are temperamental, and certain kinds of glass can block them. I'll bet the Library down there has precautions to stop people from grabbing a book, then — before their soul is taken — reading its contents off to someone listening via Lenses."

"Thanks, Bastille," I said. "You know, you're kind of useful to have around sometimes."

She smiled but then caught sight of Draulin looking at her with displeasure, and stiffened.

"So, do we camp?" Kaz asked.

I realized everyone was looking at me. "Uh, sure."

Draulin nodded, then moved over to some kind of fern-type plant and began to cut off fronds to make some shelter. It was already getting warm, but I guess that was to be expected, what with us being in Egypt and all.

I went to help Australia rifle through the packs, getting out some foodstuffs. My stomach growled as we worked; I hadn't eaten since the stale chips in the airport. "So," I said. "You're an Oculator?"

Australia flushed. "Well, not a very good one, you know. I can never really figure out how the Lenses are supposed to work."

I chuckled. "I can't either."

That only seemed to make her more embarrassed.

"What?" I asked.

She smiled in her perky way. "Nothing. I just, well. You're a natural, Alcatraz. I've tried to use Courier's Lenses a dozen times before, and you saw how poorly I managed when contacting you at the airport."

"I think you did all right," I said. "Saved *my* skin."

"I suppose," she said, looking down.

"Don't you have any Oculator's Lenses?" I asked, noticing for the first time that she wasn't wearing any Lenses. I had put back on my Oculator's Lenses after trying to contact Grandpa Smedry.

She flushed, then rifled through her pocket, eventually pulling out a pair with far more stylish frames than mine. She slid them on. "I . . . don't really like how they look."

"They're great," I said. "Look, Grandpa Smedry told me that I have to wear mine a lot to get used to them. Maybe you just need more practice."

"I've had, like, ten years."

"And how much of that did you spend wearing the Lenses?"

She thought for a moment. "Not much, I guess. Anyway, since you're here, I guess my being an Oculator isn't all that important." She smiled, but I could sense something else. She seemed good at hiding things beneath her bubbly exterior.

"I don't know about that," I said, cutting slices of bread. "*I'm* certainly glad there's another Oculator with us — especially if we have to go down into that Library."

"Why?" she said. "You're far better with Lenses than I am."

"And if we get separated?" I asked. "You could use the Courier's Lenses to contact me. Having two Oculators is never a bad thing, I've found."

"But . . . the Courier's Lenses won't work down there," she said. "That's what we just discovered."

She's right, I realized, flushing. Then, something occurred to me. I reached into one of my pockets, pulling out a pair of Lenses. "Here, try these," I said. They were yellow tinted.

She took them hesitantly, then tried them on. She blinked. "Hey!" she said. "I can see footprints."

"Tracker's Lenses," I said. "Grandpa Smedry loaned them to me. With these, you can retrace your steps back to the entrance if you get lost — or even find me by following my footprints."

Australia smiled broadly. "I've never tried a pair of these before. I can't believe they work so well!"

I didn't mention that Grandpa Smedry had said they were among the most simple of Lenses to use. "That's great," I said. "Maybe you've just always tried the wrong types of Lenses. Best to begin with the ones that work. You can borrow those."

"Thanks!" She gave me an unexpected hug, then hopped to her feet to go fetch the other pack. Smiling, I watched her go.

"You're good at that," a voice said.

I turned to find Bastille standing a short distance away. She'd cut down several long branches and was in the process of dragging them over to her mother.

"What?" I asked.

"You're good," she said. "With people, I mean."

I shrugged. "It's nothing."

"No," Bastille said. "You really made her feel better. Something had been bothering her since you arrived, but now she seems back to her old self. You kind of have a leader's flair about you, Smedry."

It makes sense, if you think about it. I had spent my entire childhood learning how to shove people away from me. I'd learned just the right buttons to push, just the right things to break, to make them hate me. Now, those same skills were coming in handy helping people feel good, rather than making them hate me.

I should have realized the trouble I was getting myself into. There's nothing worse than having people look up to you — because the more they expect, the worse you feel when you fail them. Take my advice. You don't want to be the one in charge. Becoming a leader is, in a way, like falling off a cliff. It feels like a lot of fun at first.

Then, it stops being fun. Really, really fast.

Bastille hauled the branches over to her mother, who was making a lean-to. Then, Bastille sat down beside me and took out one of our water bottles to get a drink. The water level in it didn't seem to go down at all as she gulped.

Neat, I thought.

"There's something I've been meaning to ask you," I said.

She wiped her brow. "What?"

"That jet that was chasing us," I said. "It fired a Frostbringer's Lens. I thought only Oculators could activate things like that."

She shrugged.

"Bastille," I said, eyeing her.

"You saw my mother," she grumbled. "I'm not supposed to talk about things like that."

"Why?"

"Because I'm not an Oculator."

"I'm not a pigeon either," I said. "But I can talk about feathers if I want."

She eyed me. "That's a really bad metaphor, Smedry."

"I'm good at those kind."

Feathers. Much less comfortable than scales. Glad I'm a fish instead of a bird. (You haven't forgotten about that, have you?)

"Look," I said. "What you know could be important. I . . . I think the thing that flew the jet is still alive."

"It fell from the sky!" she said.

"So did we."

"It didn't have a dragon to glide on."

"No. But it did have a face half-made from metal screws and springs."

She froze, bottle halfway to her lips.

"Ha!" I said. "You *do* know something."

"Metal face," she said. "Was it wearing a mask?"

I shook my head. "The face was *made* out of bits of metal. I saw the creature before, on the airfield. When I ran away, I felt . . . pulled backward. It was hard to move."

"Voidstormer's Lenses," she said absently. "The opposite of those Windstormer's Lenses you have."

I patted the Windstormer's Lenses in my pocket. I'd almost forgotten about those. With my last Firebringer's Lens now broken, the Windstormer's Lenses were my only real offensive Lenses. Besides them, I only had my Oculator's Lenses, my Courier's Lenses, and — of course — my Translator's Lenses.

"So, what has a metal face, flies jets, and can use Lenses?" I asked. "Sounds like a riddle."

"An easy one," Bastille said, kneeling down, speaking quietly. "Look, don't tell my mother you got this from me, but I think we're in serious trouble."

"When are we not?"

"More so now," she said. "You remember that Oculator you fought in the Library?"

"Blackburn? Sure."

"Well," she said, "he belonged to a sect of Librarians known as the Dark Oculators. There are other sects, though — four, I think — and they don't get along very well. Each sect wants to be in charge of the whole organization."

"And this guy chasing me . . . ?"

"One of the Scrivener's Bones," she said. "It's the smallest sect. Other Librarians tend to avoid the Scrivener's Bones, except when they need them, because they have . . . odd habits."

"Like?"

"Like ripping off parts of their bodies, then replacing them with Alivened materials."

I stared at her for a moment. We fish do that sometimes. We can't blink, after all. "They do *what*?"

"Just what I said," Bastille whispered. "They're part Alivened. Twisted half human, half monsters."

I shivered. We'd fought a couple of Alivened in the downtown library. Those were made of wadded-up pieces of paper, but they'd been far more dangerous than that could possibly sound. It was fighting them that lost Bastille her sword.

Alivening things — bringing inanimate objects to life with Oculatory power — is a very evil art. It requires the Oculator to give up some of his or her own humanity.

"The Scrivener's Bones usually work on commission," Bastille said. "So, another Librarian hired it."

My mother, was my immediate thought. *She's the one who hired him.* I avoided thinking about her, since doing so tended to make me sick, and there's no use being sick unless you can get out of school for it.

"He used Lenses," I said. "So this Scrivener's Bone is an Oculator?"

"Not likely," Bastille said.

"Then how?"

"There's a way to make a Lens that anyone can use," she whispered very quietly.

"There is?" I asked. "Well, why in the world don't we have more of *those*?"

Bastille glanced to the side. "Because, idiot," she hissed. "You have to sacrifice an Oculator and use his blood to forge one."

"Oh," I said.

"He was probably using a blood-forged Lens," she said, "hooked somehow into the cockpit glass so that it could fire out at us. That sounds like something the Scrivener's Bones would do. They like mixing Oculatory powers with Hushlander technology."

This talk of blood-forged Lenses should mean something to you. Finally, you may understand why I end up finding my way to an altar, about to get sacrificed. What Bastille neglected to mention was that the power of the

Oculator who was killed had a direct effect on how powerful the blood-forged Lens was. The more powerful the Oculator, the more awesome the Lens.

And I, as you might have realized, was very, very powerful.

Bastille left to cut down more branches. I sat quietly. It was probably just in my head, but I thought I could feel something off in the distance. That same dark sense I'd felt escaping from the airfield and fighting the jet.

That's silly, I told myself, shivering. *We've traveled hundreds of miles using Kaz's Talent. Even if that Scrivener's Bone did survive, it would take him days to get here.*

So I assumed.

★

A short time later I lay beneath a canopy of fronds, my black sneakers off and wrapped in my jacket to form a pillow. The others dozed, and I tried to do likewise. Yet, I couldn't stop thinking about what I'd been told.

It seemed like it all must be related somehow. The way the Lenses worked. Smedry Talents. The fact that the blood of an Oculator could make a Lens that worked for anyone. The connection between silimatic energy and Oculatory energy.

All connected. But, it was too much for me to figure out, considering the fact that I was just a fish. So, I went to sleep.

Which is pretty hard to do when you don't have eyelids.

CHAPTER 8

All right, so I'm not a fish. I admit it. What? Figured that on your own, did you? You're so clever. What gave it away? The fact that I'm writing books, the fact that I don't have fins, or the fact that I'm a downright, despicable liar?

Anyway, there *was* a purpose in that little exercise — one beyond my standard purpose. (Which is, of course, to annoy you.) I wanted to prove something. In the last chapter, I told you that I was a fish — but I also mentioned that I had black sneakers. Do you remember?

Here's the thing. That was a lie; I didn't have black sneakers. I have never owned a pair of black shoes. I was wearing white shoes; I told you about them back in Chapter One.

Why does it matter? Let's talk about something called misdirection.

In the last chapter, I told a big lie, then made you focus on it so much that you ignored the smaller lie. I said I was a fish. Then, I mentioned my black shoes in passing, so you didn't pay attention to them.

People use this strategy all the time. They drive fancy cars to distract others from their having a small house. They wear bright clothing to distract from their being — unfortunately — rather bland people. They talk really loudly to distract you from their having nothing to say.

This is what has happened to me. Everywhere I go in the Free Kingdoms, people are always excited to congratulate me, praise me, or ask for my blessing. They're all looking at the fish. They're so focused on the big thing — that I supposedly saved the world from the Librarians — that they completely ignore the facts. They don't see who I am, or what my presumed heroism cost.

So, that's why I'm writing my autobiography. I want to teach you to ignore the fish and pay attention to the shoes. Fish and shoes. Remember that.

"Alcatraz!" a voice called, waking me up. I opened bleary eyes, then sat up.

I'd been dreaming. About a wolf. A metal wolf, running, charging, getting closer.

He's coming, I thought. *The hunter. The Scrivener's Bone. He's not dead.*

"Alcatraz!" I looked toward the sound and was met by a stunning sight. My grandfather was standing just a short distance away.

"Grandpa Smedry!" I said, climbing to my feet. Indeed, it was the old man, with his bushy white mustache and tuft of white hair running around the back of his head.

"Grandpa!" I said, rushing forward. "Where have you been?!"

Grandpa Smedry looked confused, then glanced over his shoulder. He cocked his head at me. "What?"

I slowed. Why was he wearing Tracker's Lenses instead of his Oculator's Lenses? In fact, looking more closely, I saw that he had on some very odd clothing. A pink tunic and brown trousers.

"Alcatraz?" Grandpa Smedry asked. "What are you talking about?" His voice was far too feminine. In fact, it sounded just like . . .

"Australia?" I asked, stupefied.

"Oops!" he/she suddenly said, eyes opening wide. The doppelganger scrambled over to the pack and pulled out a mirror, then groaned and sat down. "Oh, Shattering Glass!"

Back under the tent, Kaz was waking up, blinking. He sat up, then began to chuckle.

"What?" I asked, looking back at him.

"My Talent," Australia said, sounding morose. "I warned you, didn't I? Sometimes, I look *really* ugly when I wake up."

"What are you saying about my grandfather?" I said, growing amused.

Australia — still looking like Grandpa — blushed. "I'm sorry," she said. "I didn't mean to say *he* was ugly. Just, well, this is ugly for me."

I held up a hand. "I understand."

"It's worse when I fall asleep thinking about someone," she said. "I was worried about him, and I guess the Talent took over. It should begin to wear off in a little bit."

I smiled, then found myself laughing at Australia's expression. I'd seen several very strange Talents in my short time with the Smedries, but until that moment, I had never run into one that I thought was more embarrassing than my own.

I would like to point out that it's not very kind to take amusement in someone else's pain. Doing so is a very bad habit — almost as bad as reading the second book in a series without having read the first.

However, it's quite different when your female cousin goes to sleep, then wakes up looking like an old man with a bushy mustache. Then it's okay to make fun of her. That happens to be one of the very few exclusions covered by the Law of Things That Are So Funny You Can't Be Blamed for Laughing at Them, No Matter What.

(Other exceptions include getting bitten by a giant penguin, falling off a giant cheese sculpture carved to look like a nose, and getting named after a prison by your parents. I have a petition in the courts to revoke that third one.)

Kaz joined me in the laughter, and eventually even Australia was chuckling. That's the way we Smedries are. If you can't laugh at your Talent, you tend to end up very grumpy.

"So, what did you want to talk to me about?" I asked Australia.

"Huh?" she asked, poking at her mustache with her finger.

"You woke me up."

Australia looked up, shocked. "Oh! Right! Um, I think I found something interesting!"

I raised an eyebrow, and she stood, rushing over to the other side of the Library's hut. She pointed at the ground.

"See!" she said.

"Dirt?" I asked.

"No, no, the footprints!"

There were no footprints in the dirt — of course, Australia was wearing the Tracker's Lenses. I reached up and tapped her Lenses.

"Oh, right!" she said, pulling off the Lenses and handing them to me.

In all fairness, you shouldn't judge Australia too harshly. She's not stupid. She just gets distracted. By, you know, breathing.

I slipped on the Lenses. There, burning on the ground, were a set of fiery white footprints. I recognized them immediately — each person leaves distinctive prints.

These belonged to my grandfather, Leavenworth Smedry. Australia herself trailed a set of puffy pink prints. Kaz's were the blue footprints, mixing with my own whitish ones, glowing in front of the hut where we'd inspected the day before. I could also see Bastille's red ones crossing the area several times, and since I hadn't known Draulin very long — and she wasn't related to me — there were only a few of her gray ones, as they disappeared rather quickly.

"See?" Australia asked again, nodding quickly. As she did so, her mustache began to fall free. "None of us gives off prints like those — though yours are close."

Kaz had joined us. "They belong to your father," I said to him.

He nodded. "Where do they lead?"

I began to walk, following the prints. Kaz and Australia followed as I made my way around the outside of the hut. Grandpa had inspected the place, just like we had. I peeked inside and noted that the prints led to one corner of the hut, then turned and walked down the stairs into the darkness.

"He went in," I said.

Kaz sighed. "So they're both down there."

I nodded. "Although, my father must have come this way too long ago for his prints to have remained. We should have thought of using the Tracker's Lenses earlier! I feel like an idiot."

Kaz shrugged. "We've found the prints. That's what's important."

"So, I did something good, right?" Australia asked.

I glanced at her. Her head had begun to sprout her normal dark hair, and her face looked like some kind of hybrid between hers and Grandpa Smedry's. While seeing her before had been amusing, now she was downright creepy.

"Um, yeah," I said. "You did a great job. I can follow these prints, and we'll find my grandfather. Then, at least, we'll know where *one* of the two of them is."

Australia nodded. Even between the times I'd glanced at her, she'd grown to look more like herself, though she seemed sad.

What? I thought. *She just made a great discovery. Without her, we wouldn't have . . .*

Australia had made the discovery because she'd had the Tracker's Lenses. Now I'd taken them back and was ready to charge off after Grandfather. I took off the Tracker's Lenses. "Why don't you keep these, Australia?"

"Really?" she said, perking up.

"Sure," I said. "You can lead us to Grandpa Smedry just as well as I can."

She smiled eagerly, taking them back. "Thank you so much!" She rushed outside, following the prints back the way they had come, apparently to see if Grandpa Smedry had visited any other places.

Kaz regarded me. "I may have misjudged you, kid."

I shrugged. "She hasn't had much luck being an Oculator. I figured I shouldn't take away the only pair of Lenses that she's been able to use effectively."

Kaz smiled, nodding in approval. "You've got a good heart. A Smedry heart. Of course, not as good as a *short person's* heart, but that's to be expected."

I raised an eyebrow.

"Reason number one hundred twenty-seven. Short people have smaller bodies, but regular-size hearts. That gives us a larger ratio of heart to flesh — making us, of course, far more compassionate than big people." He winked, then sauntered out of the room.

I shook my head, moving to follow, then stopped. I glanced at the corner, where the footprints had lead, then walked over and fished around in the dirt.

There, covered by some leaves and placed in a little hollow in the ground, was a small velvet pouch. I pulled it open and to my surprise found a pair of Lenses inside, along with a note.

Alcatraz! it read.

I was too late to stop your father from going down into the Library. I fear for the worst! He's always been the curious type and might be foolish enough to exchange his soul for information. I'm only a few days behind him, but the Library of Alexandria is a terrible maze of passages and corridors. I'm hoping that I'll be able to find him and stop him before he does anything foolish.

I'm sorry I couldn't meet you in the airport. This seemed more important. Besides, I have the feeling you can handle things on your own.

If you're reading this, then you didn't go to Nalhalla like you should have. Ha! I knew you wouldn't. You're a Smedry! I've left you a pair of Discerner's Lenses, which should be of use to you. They'll let you tell how old something is, just by looking at it.

Try not to break anything too valuable if you come down below. The Curators can be a rather unpleasant bunch. Comes from being dead, I suppose. Don't let them trick you into taking one of their books.

Love,

Grandpa Smedry

P.S. If that crazy son of mine Kazan is there, smack him on the head for me.

I lowered the note, then pulled out the Lenses. I quickly swapped them on, then glanced about the hut. They put a glow about anything I focused on — a kind of whitish shine, like you might get from sunlight reflecting off of something very pale. Except the shine was different for different objects. Most of the boards in the hut were actually downright dull, while the velvet pouch in my hand was rather bright.

Age, I thought. *They tell me how old something is — the boards were created and put there long ago. The pouch was made recently.*

I frowned to myself. Why couldn't he have left me another pair of Firebringer's Lenses? True, I'd broken the first pair — but that sort of thing tended to happen a lot around me.

The thing is, Grandpa Smedry tended to place little value on offensive Lenses. He thought information was a far better weapon.

Personally, I felt that being able to shoot superheated beams of light from your eyes was far more useful than being able to tell how old something was. But, I figured I would take what I was given.

I left the hut, walking over to the others, who were talking about Australia's discovery. They looked up as I approached, waiting for me again, like they had before.

Waiting for leadership.

Why look to me? I thought with annoyance. *I don't know what I'm doing. I don't even want to be in charge.*

"Lord Smedry," Draulin said, "should we wait for your grandfather, or should we go in after him?"

I glanced down at the pouch and was annoyed to find that the strings had unraveled as I was walking. My Talent, acting up again. "I don't know," I said.

The others looked at one another. That hadn't been the response they'd been expecting.

Grandpa Smedry obviously wanted me to lead the group down into the Library. But what if I gave the order to go down below, and something went wrong? What if someone got hurt or got captured? Wouldn't that be my fault?

But, what if my father and Grandpa Smedry really needed help?

That's the problem with being a leader. It's all about choices — and choices are *never* very much fun. If someone gives you a candy bar, you're excited. But, if someone offers you two *different* candy bars and tells you that you can only have one, what then? Whichever one you take, you'll feel that you missed out on the other one.

And I *like* candy bars. What about when you have to choose between two terrible things? Did I wait, or lead my group down into danger? That was like having to choose to either eat a tarantula or a bunch of tacks. Neither option is very appealing — both make you sick to your stomach, and both are tough to choke down without catsup.

Personally, I like it much better when someone else does the decision making. That way you have legitimate grounds to whine and complain. I tend to find both whining and complaining quite interesting and amusing, though sometimes — unfortunately — it's hard to choose which one of the two I want to do.

Sigh. Life can be so tough sometimes.

"I don't want to make that decision," I complained. "Why are you all looking at me?"

"You're the lead Oculator, Lord Smedry," Draulin said.

"Yeah, but I've only known about Oculators for three months!"

"Ah, but you're a Smedry," Kaz said.

"Yes, but . . ." I trailed off. Something was wrong. The others looked at me, but I ignored them, focusing on what I was feeling.

"What's he doing?" Australia whispered. By now, she'd gone back to looking just like her old self, though her hair was a bit messy from sleep.

"I don't know," Kaz whispered back.

"Do you think that last comment was him swearing, do you?" she whispered. "Hushlanders like to talk about posteriors. . . ."

He was coming.

I could feel it. Oculators can sense when other Oculators are using Lenses nearby. It's something built into us, just like our ability to activate Lenses.

The sense of wrongness I felt, it was like that of someone activating a Lens. But, it was twisted and dark. Frightening.

It meant someone was activating a Lens nearby that had been created in a terrible way. The hunter had found us. I spun, searching out the source of the feeling, causing the others to jump.

There he was. Standing atop a hill a short distance away, one arm too long for his body, staring down at us with his twisted face. All was silent for a moment.

Then he began to run.

Draulin cursed, whipping out her sword.

"No!" I said, running toward the hut. "We're going in!"

Draulin didn't question. She just nodded, waving for the others to go first. We dashed across the ground, Kaz pulling out a pair of Warrior's Lenses and slipping them on. His speed immediately increased, and he was able to keep up with us despite his short legs.

I reached the hut, waving Kaz and Australia inside. Bastille had taken a detour and was in the process of grabbing one of the packs.

"Bastille!" I yelled. "There isn't time!"

Draulin was backing toward us; she glanced at Bastille, then at the Scrivener's Bone. He had crossed half the distance to us, and I saw something flash in his hand. A line of whitish blue frost shot from it toward me.

I yelped, ducking into the hut. The structure shook as the burst of cold hit it, and one wall started to freeze.

Bastille skidded in a second later. "Alcatraz," she said, puffing. "I don't like this."

"What?" I asked. "Leaving your mom out there?"

"No, she can care for herself. I mean going down into the Library in a rush, without planning."

Something hit the frozen wall, and it shattered. Bastille cursed and I cried out, falling backward.

Through the opening I could see the hunter dashing toward me. After freezing the wall, he'd thrown a rock to break it.

Draulin burst in through the half-broken door. "Down!" she said, waving her sword toward the stairs, then bringing it back up to block a ray from the Frostbringer's Lens.

I glanced at Bastille.

"I've heard terrible things about this place, Alcatraz," she said.

"No time for that now," I decided, scrambling to my feet, heart thumping. I gritted my teeth, then charged down the steps toward the darkness, Bastille and Draulin following close behind.

All went black. It was like I had passed through a gateway beyond which light could not penetrate. I felt a sudden dizziness, and I fell to my knees.

"Bastille?" I called into the darkness.

No response.

"Kaz! Australia! Draulin!"

My voice didn't even echo back to me.

I'll take one chocolate bar and a handful of tacks, please. Anyone got any catsup?

CHAPTER 9

I would like to try an experiment. Get out some paper and write a 0 on it. Then I want you to go down a line and put a 0 there. You see, the 0 is a magic number, as it is — well — 0. You can't get better than that! Now, on the next one, 0 isn't enough. 7 is the number to put here. Why isn't the 0 good enough here? 0 is not magical now. Once great, the 0 has been reduced to being nonsense. Now, take your paper and throw it away, then turn this book sideways.

Look closely at the paragraph above this one. (Or, uh, I guess since you turned the book sideways it's the paragraph *beside* this one.) Regardless, you might be able to see a face in the numbers in the paragraph — 0s form the eyes, the 7 is a nose, and a line of 0s form the mouth. It's smiling at you because you're holding your book sideways, and — as everyone knows — that's not the way to read books. In fact, how are you reading this paragraph, anyway? Turn the book around. You look silly.

Oh, very clever. Now you've got it upside down.

There. That's better. Anyway, I believe I talked in my last book about how first impressions are often wrong. You may have had the impression that I was done talking about first impressions. You were wrong. Imagine that.

There's so much more to be learned here. It's not just people's *first* impressions that are often wrong. Many of the ideas we have thought and believed for a long time are, in fact, dead wrong. For instance, I believed for years that Librarians were my friends. Some people believe that asparagus tastes good. Others don't buy this book because they think it won't be interesting.

Wrong, wrong, and so wrong. In my experience, I've found it best not to judge what I *think* I'm seeing until I've had enough time to study and learn. Something that appears to make no sense may, actually, be brilliant. (Like my art in paragraph one.)

Remember that. It might be important somewhere else in this book.

I forced myself to my feet in the complete darkness. I looked about, but of course that did no good. I called out again. No response.

I shivered in the darkness. Now, it wasn't just dark down there. It was *dark*. Dark like I'd been swallowed by a whale, then that whale had been eaten by a bigger whale, then that bigger whale had gotten lost in a deep cave, which had then been thrown into a black hole.

It was so dark I began to fear that I'd been struck blind. I was therefore overjoyed when I caught a glimmer of light. I turned toward it, relieved.

"Thank the first sands," I exclaimed. "It's —"

I choked off. The light was coming from the flames burning in the sockets of a bloodred skull.

I cried out, stumbling away, and my back hit a rough, dusty wall. I moved along it, scrambling in the darkness, but ran forehead first into another wall at the corner. Trapped, I spun around, watching the skull grow closer. The fires in its eyes soon illuminated the creature's robe-like cloak and thin skeleton arms. The whole body — skull, cloak, even the flames — seemed faintly translucent.

I had met my first Curator of Alexandria. I fumbled, reaching into my jacket, remembering for the first time that I was carrying Lenses. Unfortunately, in the darkness, I couldn't tell which pocket was which, and I was too nervous to count properly.

I pulled out a random pair of spectacles, hoping I'd grabbed the Windstormer's Lenses. I shoved them on.

The Curator glowed with a whitish light. *Great,* I thought. *I know how old it is. Maybe I can bake it a birthday cake.*

The Curator said something to me, but it was in a strange, raspy language that I didn't understand.

"Uh . . . I missed that . . . ," I said, fumbling for a different pair of Lenses. "Could you repeat yourself . . . ?"

It spoke again, getting closer. I whipped out another pair of Lenses and put them on, focusing on the creature and hoping to blow it backward with a gust of wind. I was pretty sure I'd gotten the right pocket this time.

I was wrong, of course.

". . . visitor to the great Library of Alexandria," the thing hissed, "you must pay the price of entry."

The Lenses of Rashid — Translator's Lenses. Now, not only did I know how old it was, I could understand its demonic voice as it sucked out my soul. I made a mental note to speak sternly with my grandfather about the kinds of Lenses he gave me.

"The price," the creature said, stepping up to me.

"Uh . . . I seem to have left my wallet outside . . . ," I said, fumbling in my jacket for another pair of Lenses.

"Cash does not interest us," another voice whispered.

I glanced to the side, where another Curator — with burning eyes and a red skull — was floating toward me. With the extra light, I could see that neither creature had legs. Their cloaks just kind of trailed off into nothingness at the bottoms.

"Then, what do you want?" I asked, gulping.

"We want . . . your paper."

I blinked. "Excuse me?"

"Anything you have written down," a third creature said, approaching. "All who enter the Library of Alexandria must give up their books, their notes, and their writings so that we may copy them and add them to our collection."

"Okay . . . ," I said. "That sounds fair enough."

My heart continued to race, as if it refused to believe that a bunch of undead monsters with flames for eyes weren't going to kill me. I pulled out everything I had — which only included the note from Grandpa Smedry, a gum wrapper, and a few American dollars.

They took it all, plucking them from me and leaving my hands feeling icy and cold. Curators, it might be noted, give off a freezing chill. Because of this, they never need ice for their drinks. Unfortunately, since they're undead spirits, they can't really drink soda. It's one of the great ironies of our world.

"That's all I have," I said, shrugging.

"Liar," one hissed.

That isn't the type of thing one likes to hear from undead spirits. "No," I said honestly. "That's it!"

I felt the freezing hands on my body, and I cried out. Despite looking translucent, the things had quite firm grips. They spun me about, then ripped the tag from my shirt and from my jeans.

Then, they just backed away. "You want *those*?" I asked.

"All writing must be surrendered," one of the creatures said. "The purpose of the Library is to collect all knowledge ever written down."

"Well, you won't get there very fast by copying down the tags off T-shirts," I grumbled.

"Do not question our methods, mortal."

I shivered, realizing it probably wasn't a good idea to sass the soul-sucking monster with a burning skull for a head. In that way, soul-sucking monsters with burning skulls are a lot like teachers. (I understand your confusion; I get them mixed up too.)

With that, the three spirits began to drift away.

"Wait," I said, anxious not to return to the darkness. "What about my friends? Where are they?"

One of the spirits turned back. "They have been separated from you. All must be alone when they enter the Library." It drifted closer. "Have you come seeking knowledge? We can provide it for you. Anything you wish. Any book, any volume, any tome. Anything that has been written, we can provide. You need but ask. . . ."

The robed body and burning skull drifted around me, voice subtle and inviting as it whispered. "You can know anything. Including, perhaps, where your father is."

I spun toward the creature. "You know that?"

"We can provide some information," it said. "You need but ask to check out the volume."

"And the cost?"

The skull seemed to smile, if that was possible. "Cheap."

"My soul?"

The smile deepened.

"No, thank you," I said, shuddering.

"Very well," the Curator said, drifting away.

Suddenly, lamps on the walls flickered to life, lighting the room. The lamps were little oil-filled containers that looked like the kind you'd expect a genie to hold in an old Arabian story. I didn't really care; I was just glad for the light. By it, I could see that I stood in a dusty room with old brick walls. There were several hallways leading away from the room, and there were no doors in the doorways.

Great, I thought. *Of all the times to give away my Tracker's Lenses . . .*

I picked a door at random and walked out into the hallway, immediately struck by how vast it was. It seemed to extend forever. Lamps hung from pillars that — extending into the distance — looked like a flickering, haunting runway on a deserted airfield. To my right and to my left were shelves filled with scrolls.

There were thousands upon thousands of them, all with the same dusty, catacomb-like feel. I felt a little bit daunted. Even my own footsteps sounded too loud as they echoed in the vast chamber.

I continued for a time, stepping softly, studying the rows and rows of cobwebbed scrolls. It was as if I were in a massive crypt — except, instead of bodies, this was the place where manuscripts were placed to die.

"They seem endless," I whispered to myself, looking up. The pockets of scrolls reached all the way up the walls to the ceiling some twenty feet above. "I wonder how many there are."

"You could know, if you wanted," a voice whispered. I spun to find a Curator hovering behind me. How long had it been there?

"We have a list," it whispered, floating closer, its skull face looking more shadowed now that there was external light. "You could read it, if you want. Check it out from the Library."

"No, thank you," I said, backing away.

The Curator remained where it was. It didn't make any threatening moves, so I continued onward, occasionally glancing over my shoulder.

You may be wondering how the Curators can claim to have every book ever written. I have it on good authority that they have many means of locating books and adding them to their collection. For instance, they have a tenuous deal with the Librarians who control the Hushlands.

In the United States alone, there are thousands upon thousands of books published every year. Most of these are either "literature," books about people who don't do anything, or they are silly fiction works about dreadfully dull topics, such as dieting.

(There *is* a purpose to all of these useless books produced in America. They are, of course, intended to make people self-conscious about themselves so that the Librarians can better control them. The quickest way I've found to feel bad about yourself is to read a self-help book, and the second quickest is to read a depressing literary work intended to make you feel terrible about humanity in general.)

Anyway, the point is that the Librarians publish hundreds of thousands of books each year. What happens to all of these books? Logically, we should all be overwhelmed by them. Buried in a tsunami of texts, gasping for breath as we drown in an endless sea of stories about girls with eating disorders.

The answer is the Library of Alexandria. The Librarians ship their excess books there in exchange for the promise that the Curators won't go out into the Hushlands and seek the volumes themselves. It's really a shame. After all, the

Curators — being skeletons — could probably teach us a few things about dieting.

I continued to wander the musty halls of the Library, feeling rather small and insignificant compared with the massive pillars and rows and rows and rows and rows and rows and rows and rows and rows and rows and rows and rows and rows of books.

Occasionally, I passed other hallways that branched off the first. They looked identical to the one I was walking in, and I soon realized that I had no idea which way I was going. I glanced backward, and was disappointed to realize that the only place in the Library that seemed clean of dust was the floor. There would be no footprints to guide me back the way I had come, and I had no bread crumbs to leave as a trail. I considered using belly-button lint, but decided that would not only be gross, but wasteful as well. (Do you have any idea how much that stuff is worth?)

Besides, there wouldn't be much point in leaving a trail in the first place. I didn't know where I was going, true, but I also didn't know where I'd been. I sighed. "I don't suppose there's a map of this place anywhere?" I asked, turning back to the Curator who followed a short distance behind.

"Of course there is," he said in a phantom voice.

"Really? Where is it?"

"I can fetch it for you." The skull smiled. "You'll have to check it out, though."

"Great," I said flatly. "I can give you my soul to discover the way out, then not be able to *use* the way out because you'd own my soul."

"Some have done so before," the ghost said. "Traveling the library stacks can be maddening. To many, it is worth the cost of their soul to finally see the solution."

I turned away. The Curator, however, continued talking. "In fact, you'd be surprised the people who come here, searching for the solutions to simple puzzles." The creature's voice grew louder as it spoke, and it floated closer to me. "Some old women grow very attached to a modern diversion known as the 'Crossword Puzzle.' We've had several come here, looking for answers. We have their souls now."

I frowned, eyeing the thing.

"Many would rather give up what remains of their lives than live in ignorance," it said. "This is only one of the many ways that we gain souls. In truth, some do not care which book they get, for once they become one of us, they can read other books in the Library. By then, of course, their soul is bound here, and they can never leave or share that knowledge. However, the endless knowledge appeals to them."

Why was it talking so loudly? It seemed to be pushing up against me a bit, its coldness prodding me on. As if it were trying to force me to walk faster.

In a moment I realized what was going on. The Curator was a fish. If that were the case, what were the shoes? (Metaphorically speaking, of course. Read back a few chapters if you've forgotten.)

I closed my eyes, focusing. There, I heard it. A quiet voice, calling for help. It sounded like Bastille.

I snapped my eyes open and ran down a side hallway. The ghost cursed in an obscure language — my Translator's Lenses kindly let me know the meaning of the word, and I will be equally kind here in not repeating it, since it involved eggbeaters — and followed me.

I found her hanging from the ceiling between two pillars in the hallway, letting out a few curses of her own. She was tangled up in a strange network of ropes; some of them twisted around her legs, others held her arms. It seemed that her struggles were only making things worse.

"Bastille?" I asked.

She stopped struggling, silver hair hanging down around her face. "Smedry?"

"How did you get up there?" I asked, noticing a Curator hanging in the air upside down beside her. Its robe didn't seem to respond to gravity — but, then, that's rather common for ghosts, I would think.

"Does it matter?" Bastille snapped, flailing about, apparently trying to shake herself free.

"Stop struggling. You're only making it worse."

She huffed, but stopped.

"Are you going to tell me what happened?" I asked.

"Trap," she said, twisting about a bit. "I triggered a trip wire, and the next moment I was hanging up here. If that wasn't bad enough, the burning-eyed freak here keeps whispering to me that he can give me a book that will show me how to escape. It'll just cost my soul!"

"Where's your dagger?" I asked.

"In my pack."

I saw it on the floor a short distance away. I walked over, watching out for trip wires. Inside, I found her crystalline dagger, along with some foodstuffs and — I was surprised to remember — the boots with Grappler's Glass on the bottoms. I smiled.

"I'll be right there," I said, putting the boots on and activating the glass. Then, I proceeded to try walking up the side of the wall.

If you've never attempted this, I heartily recommend it. There's a very nice rush of wind, accompanied by an inviting feeling of vertigo, as you fall backward and hit the ground. You also look something like an idiot — but for most of us, that's nothing new.

"What are you *doing*?" Bastille asked.

"Trying to walk up to you," I said, sitting up and rubbing my head.

"Grappler's Glass, Smedry. It only sticks to other pieces of glass."

Ah, right, I thought. Now, this might have seemed like a very stupid thing to forget, but you can't blame me. I was suffering from having fallen to the ground and a hit to the head, after all.

"Well, how am I going to get up to you, then?"

"You could just throw me the dagger."

I looked up skeptically. The ropes seemed wound pretty tightly around her. They, however, were connected to the pillars.

"Hang on," I said, walking up to one of the pillars.

"Alcatraz . . . ," she said, sounding uncertain. "What are you doing?"

I laid my hand against the pillar, then closed my eyes. I'd destroyed the jet by just touching the smoke . . . could I do something like that here too? Guide my Talent up the pillar to the ropes?

"Alcatraz!" Bastille said. "I don't want to get squished by a bunch of falling pillars. Don't . . ."

I released a burst of breaking power.

"Gak!"

She said this last part as her ropes — which were connected to the pillars — frayed and fell to pieces. I opened my eyes in time to see her grab the one remaining whole piece of rope and swing down to the ground, landing beside me, puffing slightly.

She looked up. The pillar didn't fall on us. I removed my hand.

She cocked her head, then regarded me. "Huh."

"Not bad, eh?"

She shrugged. "A real man would have climbed up and cut me down with the dagger. Come on. We've got to find the others."

I rolled my eyes, but took her thank-you for what it was

worth. I walked over as she stuffed the boots and dagger back in her pack, then threw it over her shoulder. We walked down the hallway for a moment, then spun as we heard a crashing sound.

The pillar had finally decided to topple over, throwing up broken chips of stone as it hit the ground. The entire hallway shook from the impact.

A wave of dust from the rubble puffed over us. Bastille gave me a suffering look, then sighed and continued walking.

CHAPTER 10

You may wonder why I hate fantasy novels so much. Or, maybe you don't. That doesn't really matter, because I'm going to tell you anyway.

(Of course, if you want to know how the book ends, you could just skip to the last page — but I wouldn't recommend that. It will prove very disturbing to your psyche.)

Anyway, let's talk about fantasy novels. First, you have to understand that when I say "fantasy novels," I mean books about dieting or literature or people living during the Great Depression. Fantasy novels, then, are books that don't include things like glass dragons, ghostly Curators, or magical Lenses.

I hate fantasy novels. Well, that's not true. I don't actually really *hate* them. I just get annoyed by what they've done to the Hushlands.

People don't read anymore. And, when they do, they don't read books like this one, but instead read books that depress them, because those books are seen as important. Somehow, the Librarians have sucessfully managed to convince most people in the Hushlands that they shouldn't read anything that isn't boring.

It comes down to Biblioden the Scrivener's great vision for the world — a vision in which people never do anything abnormal, never dream, and never experience anything strange. His minions teach people to stop reading fun books, and instead focus on fantasy novels. That's what I call them, because those books keep people trapped. Keep them inside the nice little fantasy that they consider to be the "real" world. A fantasy that tells them they don't need to try something new.

After all, trying new things can be difficult.

"We need a plan," Bastille said as we walked the corridors of the Library. "We can't just keep wandering around in here."

"We need to find Grandpa Smedry," I said, "or my father."

"We also need to find Kaz and Australia, not to mention my mother." She grimaced a bit at that last part.

And . . . that's not everything either, I thought. *My father came here for a reason. He came searching for something.*

Something very important.

I'd found a communication from him several months back — it had come with the package that had contained the Sands of Rashid. My father had sounded tense in his letter. He'd been excited, but worried too.

He'd discovered something dangerous. The Sands of Rashid — the Translator's Lenses — had only been the beginning. They were a step toward uncovering something much greater. Something that had frightened my father.

He'd spent thirteen years searching for whatever the something was. That trail had ended here, at the Library of Alexandria. Could he really have come because he'd grown frustrated? Had he traded his soul for the answers he sought, just so that he could finally stop searching?

I shivered, glancing at the Curators, who floated behind us. "Bastille," I said. "You said that one of them spoke to you?"

"Yeah," she said. "Kept trying to get me to borrow a book."

"It spoke to you in English?"

"Well, Nalhallan," she said. "But it's pretty much the same thing. Why?"

"Mine spoke to me in a language I didn't understand."

"Mine did that at first too," she said. "Several of them surrounded me and searched through my possessions. They grabbed the supply list and several of the labels off of the foodstuffs. Then, they left — all except for that one behind us. It continued to jabber at me in that infuriating language. It was only after I'd been caught that it started speaking Nalhallan."

I glanced again at the Curators. *They use traps,* I thought. *But not ones that kill — ones that keep people tangled up. They separate everyone who comes in, then they make each one wander the hallways, lost. They talk to us in a language they know we don't understand when they could easily speak in English instead.*

This whole place is all about annoying people. The Curators are trying to make us frustrated. All so that we'll give up and take one of the books they're offering.

"So," Bastille said. "What's our plan?"

I shrugged. "Why ask me?"

"Because you're in charge, Alcatraz," she said, sighing. "What's your problem, anyway? Half the time you seem ready to give orders and charge about. The other half of the time, you complain that you don't want to be the one who has to make the decisions."

I didn't answer. To be honest, I hadn't really figured out my feelings either.

"Well?" she asked.

"First, we find Kaz, Australia, and your mother."

"Why would you need to find me?" Kaz asked. "I mean, I'm right here."

We both jumped. And, of course, there he was. Wearing his bowler and rugged jacket, hands in his pockets, smiling at us impishly.

"Kaz!" I said. "You found us!"

"You were lost," he said, shrugging. "If I'm lost, it's easier for me to find someone else who is lost — since abstractly, we're both in the same place."

I frowned, trying to make sense of that. Kaz looked around, eyeing the pillars and their archways. "Not at all like I imagined it."

"Really?" Bastille asked. "It looks pretty much like I figured it would."

"I expected them to take better care of their scrolls and books," Kaz said.

"Kaz," I said. "You found us, right?"

"Uh, what did I just say, kid?"

"Can you find Australia too?"

He shrugged. "I can try. But, we'll have to be careful. Quite nearly got myself caught in a trap a little ways back. I tripped a wire, and a large hoop swung out of the wall and tried to grab me."

"What happened?" Bastille said.

He laughed. "It went right over my head. Reason number fifteen, Bastille: Short people make smaller targets!"

I just shook my head.

"I'll scout ahead," Bastille said. "Looking for trip wires. Then the two of you can follow. Kaz will engage his Talent at each intersection and pick the next way to go. Hopefully, his Talent will lead us to Australia."

"Sounds like a good enough plan for now," I said.

Bastille put on her Warrior's Lenses, then took off, moving very carefully down the hallway. Kaz and I were left standing there with nothing to do.

Something occurred to me. "Kaz," I said. "How long did it take you to learn to use your Talent?"

"Ha!" he said. "You make it sound like I *have* learned to use it, kid."

"But, you're better with yours than I am with mine." I glanced back at the rubbled pillar, which was still visible in the distance behind us.

"Talents are tough, I'll admit," he said, following my gaze. "You do that?"

I nodded.

"You know, it was the sound of that pillar falling that let me know I was close to you. Sometimes, what looks like a mistake turns out to be kind of useful."

"I know that, but I still have trouble. Every time I think I've got my Talent figured out, I break something I didn't intend to."

The shorter man leaned against a pillar on the side of the hallway. "I know what you mean, Al. I spent most of my youth getting lost. I couldn't be trusted to go to the bathroom on my own because I'd end up in Mexico. Once, I stranded your father and myself on an island alone for two weeks because I couldn't figure out how to make the blasted Talent work."

He shook his head. "The thing is, the more powerful a Talent is, the harder it is to control. You and I — like your father and grandfather — have prime Talents. Right on the Incarnate Wheel, fairly pure. They're bound to give us lots of trouble."

I cocked my head. "Incarnate Wheel?"

He seemed surprised. "Nobody's explained it to you?"

"The only one I've really talked to about Talents is my grandfather."

"Yeah, but what about in school?"

"Ah . . . no," I said. "I went to Librarian school, Kaz. I did hear a lot about the Great Depression, though."

Kaz snorted. "Fantasy books. Those Librarians . . ." He sighed, squatting down by the floor and pulling out a stick. He grabbed a handful of dust from the corner, threw it out on the floor, then drew a circle in it.

"There have been a *lot* of Smedries over the centuries," he said, "and a lot of Talents. Many of them tend to be similar, in the long run. There are four kinds: Talents that affect space, time, knowledge, and the physical world." He drew a circle in the dust, then split it into four pieces.

"Take my Talent, for instance," he continued. "I change things in space. I can get lost, then get found again."

"What about Grandpa Smedry?"

"Time," Kaz said. "He arrives late to things. Australia, however, has a Talent that can change the physical world — in this case, her own shape." He wrote her name in the dust on the wheel. "Her Talent is fairly specific, and not as broad as your grandfather's. For instance, there was a Smedry a couple of centuries back who could look ugly *any* time he wanted, not just when he woke up in the morning. Others have been able to change anyone's appearance, not just their own. Understand?"

I shrugged. "I guess so."

"The closer the Talent gets to its purest form, the more powerful it is," Kaz said. "Your grandfather's Talent is very pure — he can manipulate time in a lot of different circumstances. Your father and I have very similar Talents — I can get lost and Attica can lose things — and both are flexible. Siblings often have similar powers."

"What about Sing?" I asked.

"Tripping. That's what we call a knowledge Talent — he knows how to do something normal with extraordinary ability. Like Australia, though, his power isn't very flexible. In that case, we put them at the edge of the wheel near the rim. Talents like my father's, which are more powerful, we place closer to the center."

I nodded slowly. "So . . . what does this have to do with me?"

Bastille had returned, and was watching with interest.

"Well, it's hard to say," Kaz said. "You're getting into some deep philosophy now, kid. There are those who argue that the Breaking Talent is simply a physical-world Talent, but one that is very versatile and very powerful."

He met my eyes, then poked his stick into the very center of the circle. "There are others who argue that the Breaking Talent is much more. It seems to be able to do things that affect all four areas. Legends say that one of your ancestors — one of only two others to have this Talent — broke time and space together, forming a little bubble where nothing aged.

"Other records speak of breakings equally marvelous. Breakings that change people's memory or their abilities. What is it to 'break' something? What can you change? How far can the Talent go?"

He raised his stick, pointing at me. "Either way, kid, *that's* why it's so hard for you to control. To be honest, even after centuries of studying them, we really don't understand the Talents. I don't know that we ever will, though your father was very keen on trying."

Kaz stood up, dusting off his hands. "And that's why he came here, I guess."

"How do you know so much?" I asked.

Kaz raised an eyebrow. "What? You think I spend all my time making up witty lists and getting lost on my way to the bathroom? I have a job, kid."

"Lord Kazan's a scholar," Bastille said. "Focusing on arcane theory."

"Great," I said, rolling my eyes. "Another professor." After Grandpa Smedry, Sing, and Quentin, I was half convinced that everyone who lived in the Free Kingdoms was one kind of academic or another.

Kaz shrugged. "It's a Smedry trait, kid. We tend to be very interested in information. Either way, your father was the real genius — I'm just a humble philosopher. Bastille, how's the pathway up ahead look?"

"Clean," she said. "No trip wires that I found."

"Great," he said.

"You actually seem a bit disappointed."

Kaz shrugged. "Traps are interesting. They're always a surprise, kind of like presents on your birthday."

"Except these presents might decapitate you," Bastille said flatly.

"All part of the fun, Bastille."

She sighed, shooting me a glance over her sunglasses. *Smedries,* it seemed to say. *All the same.*

I smiled at her, and nodded for us to get moving. Kaz took the lead. As we walked, I noticed that a couple of Curators were busy copying down Kaz's drawing. I turned away, then jumped as I found a Curator hanging beside me.

"The Incarna knew about Smedry Talents," the thing whispered. "We have a book here, one of theirs, written millennia ago. It explains exactly where the Talents first came from. We have one of only two copies that still exist."

It hovered closer.

"You can have it," the creature whispered. "Check it out, if you wish."

I snorted. "I'm not *that* curious. I'd be a fool to give you my soul for information I could never use."

"Ah, but maybe you *could* use it," the Curator said. "What could you accomplish if you understood your Talent, young Smedry? Would you, perhaps, have enough skill to gain your freedom from us? Get your soul back? *Break* out of our prison . . ."

This gave me pause. It made a twisted, frightening sense. Maybe I *could* trade my soul away, then learn how to free myself using the book I gained. "It's possible, then?"

I asked. "Someone could break free after having been turned into a Curator?"

"Anything is possible," the creature whispered, focusing its burning sockets on me. "Why don't you try? You could learn so much. Things people haven't known for millennia . . ."

It is a testament to the subtle trickery of the Curators that I actually thought, for just a moment, about trading my soul for a book on arcane theory.

And then I came to my senses. I couldn't even control my Talent as it was. What made me think that I, of all people, would be able to use it to outsmart a group as ancient and powerful as the Curators of Alexandria?

I chuckled and shook my head, causing the Curator to back away in obvious displeasure. I hurried my pace, catching up with the others. Kaz walked in front, leading us as he had before, letting his Talent lose us and carry us toward Australia. Theoretically.

Indeed, as I walked, I swore that I could see the stacks of scrolls changing around us. It wasn't that they transformed or anything — yet, if I glanced at a stack, then turned away, then glanced back, I couldn't tell if it was actually the same one or not. Kaz's Talent was carrying us through the corridors without our being able to feel the change.

Something occurred to me. "Kaz?"

The short man looked back, raising an eyebrow.

"So . . . your Talent has lost us, right?"

"Yup," he said.

"As we walk, we're moving through the Library, hopping to different points, even though we feel like we're just walking down a corridor."

"You've got it, kid. I've got to tell you — you're smarter than you look."

I frowned. "So, what exactly was the purpose of having Bastille scout ahead? Didn't we leave that corridor behind the moment you turned on your Talent?"

Kaz froze.

At that moment, I heard something click beneath me. I looked down with shock to see that I'd stepped directly onto a trip wire.

"Ah, wing nuts," Kaz swore.

CHAPTER 11

I must apologize for the beginning of that last chapter. My goal is to write a completely frivolous book, for if I actually say anything important, I run the risk of making people worship or respect me even more. Therefore, I should ask that you will do me a favor. Get out some scissors, and cut out the next few paragraphs in this chapter. Paste them over the beginning of the last chapter, hiding it away so that you never have to read its pretentious editorializing again.

Ready? Go.

Once there was a bunny. This bunny had a birthday party. It was the bestest birthday party ever. Because that was the day the bunny got a bazooka.

The bunny loved his bazooka. He blew up all sorts of things on the farm. He blew up the stable of Henrietta the Horse. He blew up the pen of Pugsly the Pig. He blew up the coop of Chuck the Chicken.

"I have the bestest bazooka ever," the bunny said. Then the farm friends proceeded to beat him senseless and steal his bazooka. It was the happiest day of his life.

The end.

Epilogue: Pugsly the Pig, now without a pen, was quite annoyed. When none of the others were looking, he stole the bazooka. He tied a bandana on his head and swore vengeance for what had been done to him.

"From this day on," he whispered, raising the bazooka, "I shall be known as *Hambo*."

There. I feel much better. Now we can return to the story, refreshed and confident that you're reading the right kind of book.

I cringed, tense, looking down at my foot on the trip wire. "So," I said, glancing at Bastille, "is it going to do any —

"Gak!"

At that moment, panels on the ceiling fell away, dumping what seemed like a thousand buckets full of dark, sticky sludge on us. I tried to move out of the way, but I was far too slow. Even Bastille, with her enhanced Crystin speed, couldn't dodge fast enough.

It hit, covering us in a tarlike substance. I tried to yell, but the sound came out in a gurgle as the thick, black material got into my mouth. It had a rather unpleasant flavor. Kind of like a cross between bananas and tar, heavy on the tar.

I struggled and was frustrated to feel the goop suddenly harden. I was frozen in place, one eye open, the other closed, my mouth filled with hard tar, my nose — fortunately — unplugged.

"Great," Bastille said. I could just barely see her, covered in hardened sludge a short distance away, stuck in a running posture. She'd had the sense to shade her face, so her eyes and mouth were uncovered — but her arm was glued to her forehead. "Kaz, you stuck too?"

"Yeah," said a muffled voice. "I tried to lose myself, but it didn't work. We were already lost."

"Alcatraz?" Bastille asked.

I made a grumbling noise through my nose.

"He looks all right," Kaz said. "He isn't going to be waxing eloquent anytime soon, though."

"As if he ever does," Bastille said, struggling.

Enough of this, I thought in annoyance, releasing my Talent into the goop. Nothing happened. There are, unfortunately, plenty of things that are resistant to Smedry Talents.

Several Curators glided across the floor to us, looking quite pleased with themselves. "We can provide a book for you that will explain how to get out," one said.

"You will find it very interesting," said another.

"Shatter yourselves," Bastille snapped, grunting again as she tried to get free. Nothing moved but her chin.

"What kind of offer is that?" Kaz demanded. "We wouldn't be able to read the book like this!"

"We'd be happy to read it to you," one of the others said. "So that you would understand how to escape in the moments before your soul was taken."

"Plus," another whispered, "you would have all of eternity to study. Surely that must appeal to you, a scholar. An eternity with the knowledge of the Library. All at your fingertips."

"Never able to leave," Kaz said. "Trapped forever in this pit, forced to entice others into the trap."

"Your brother thought the trade worthwhile," one of them whispered.

What! I thought. *Father!*

"You lie," Kaz said. "Attica would never fall for one of your tricks!"

"We didn't have to trick him," another whispered, floating close to me. "He came quite willingly. All for a book. A single, special book."

"What book?" Bastille asked.

The Curators fell silent, skull heads smiling. "Will you trade your soul for that knowledge?"

Bastille began to swear, struggling harder. The Curators moved around her, speaking in a language that my Lenses told me was classical Greek.

If I could just get to my Windstormer's Lenses, I thought. *Perhaps I could blow some of this goop away.*

I couldn't even wiggle my fingers, though, let alone reach into my jacket.

If only my Talent would work! I focused, drawing forth all of the power I could, and released it into the goop. Yet, it refused to break or yield.

Something occurred to me. The goop was resistant, but what about the floor beneath me? I gathered my Talent again, then released it downward.

I strained, feeling the pulsings of energy run through my body and out my feet. I felt my shoes unravel, the rubber slipping free, the canvas falling apart. I felt the rock

beneath my heels crumble. But, that was ultimately useless, since my body was still held tightly by the goop. The
ground fell away beneath me, but I didn't fall with it.

The Curator closest to me turned. "Are you certain you
don't want that book on Talents, young Oculator? Perhaps
it would help you free yourself."

Focus, I thought as the rest of the Curators continued
to torment Bastille. *They said that there's a book on how to
escape this goop. Well, that means there's a way out.*

I continued struggling, but that was obviously useless.
If it was possible to break free with just muscles, then
Bastille would manage to long before I did.

So, instead, I focused on the goop itself. What could I
determine about it? The stuff in my mouth seemed slightly
softer than the stuff around the outside of my body. Was
there a reason for that? Spit, perhaps? Maybe the goop
didn't harden when it was wet.

I began to drool out some saliva, trying to get it on the
goop. Spit began to seep out of the top of my mouth, and
down the front of the glob of goop on my face.

"Uh . . . Alcatraz?" Bastille asked. "You all right?"

I tried to grunt in a reassuring way. But, then, I've found
that it's very hard to grunt eloquently when you're spitting.

After several minutes, I came to the unpleasant conclusion that the goop didn't dissolve in saliva. Unfortunately, now I was not only being held tightly by a sheet of hardened black tar, I'd also drooled all over the front of my shirt.

"Getting frustrated?" a Curator asked, hovering around me in a circle. "How long will you struggle? You need not be able to speak. Simply blink three times if you want to trade your soul for the way out."

I kept my eyes wide open. They began to dry out, which was appropriately ironic, considering the state of my shirt.

The Curator looked disappointed, but continued to hover. *Why bother with all of the cajoling?* I wondered. *We're in their power. Why not kill us? Why not just take our souls from us by force?*

That thought made me pause. If they hadn't done that already, then it probably meant that they *couldn't*. Which seemed to imply that they were bound by some kind of laws or a code or something.

My jaw was getting tired. It seemed an odd thing to think of. I was being held tightly in all places, and I was worried about my jaw? Was that because it wasn't being held as tightly as the rest? But, I'd already determined that. The goop in my mouth wasn't as hard.

So, uncertain what else to do, I bit down. Hard. Surprisingly, my teeth cut through the stuff, and the chunk of goop came off in my mouth. Suddenly, the entire blanket of it — the stuff covering me, Bastille, Kaz, and the floor — shuddered.

What? I thought. The stuff I'd bitten off immediately became liquid again, and I nearly choked as I was forced to swallow it. The piece in front of my face withdrew slightly after the bite, and I could still see it wiggling. Almost as if . . . the entire blob were alive.

I shivered. Yet, I didn't have many options. Wiggling my head a bit — it was looser now that the stuff had retreated from my face — I snapped forward and took another bite out of the stuff. It shook and pulled farther away. I leaned over, and — spitting out the chunk of tarry-bananaish stuff — I took another bite.

The blanket of goop pulled back from me completely, like a shy dog that had been kicked. The metaphor seemed apt, and so I kicked it.

The blob shook, then retreated off of Bastille and Kaz, fleeing away down the corridor. I spit a few times, grimacing at the taste. Then I eyed the Curators. "Perhaps you should train your traps a little better."

They did not look pleased. Kaz, on the other hand, was smiling widely. "Kid, I'm almost tempted to make you an official short person!"

"Thanks," I said.

"Course, we'd have to cut your legs off at the knees," Kaz said. "But that would be a small price to pay!" He winked at me. I'm pretty sure that was a joke.

I shook my head, stepping out of the rubbled pocket I'd made in the floor with my Talent. My shoes barely hung to my feet, and I kicked them off, forced to walk barefoot.

Still, I'd gotten us free. I turned, smiling, to Bastille. "Well, I believe that makes *two* traps I've saved you from."

"Oh?" she said. "And are we going to start a count of the ones you got me *into*, as well? Who was it who stepped on that trip wire again?"

I flushed.

"Any one of us could have tripped it, Bastille," Kaz said, walking up to us. "As fun as that was, I'm starting to think it might be a good idea if we didn't hit any more of those. We need to go more carefully."

"You think?" Bastille asked flatly. "The trick is, I can't scout ahead. Not if you're leading us with your Talent."

"We'll just have to be more cautious, then," Kaz said. I looked down at the trip wire, thinking about the danger. We couldn't afford to stumble into every one of those we came across. Who knew if we'd even be able to think of a way out of the next one?

"Kaz, Bastille, wait a second." I reached into a pocket, pulling out my Lenses. I left the Windstormer's Lenses alone and put on the Discerner's Lenses — the ones that Grandpa Smedry had left for me up above.

Immediately, everything around me began to give off a faint glow, indicating how old it was. I looked down. Sure enough, the trip wire glowed far lighter than the stones or the scrolls around it. It was newer than the original construction of the building. I looked up, smiling. "I think I've found a way around the problem."

"Are those Discerner's Lenses?" Bastille asked.

I nodded.

"Where in the sands did you get a pair of those?"

"Grandpa Smedry left them for me," I said. "Outside, along with a note." I frowned, glancing at the Curators. "Speaking of which, didn't you say you'd return the writings you took from me?"

The creatures glanced at one another. Then, one of them approached, betraying a sullen look. The apparition bent down and set some things on the ground: copies of my tags, the wrapper that had been taken from me, and Grandpa Smedry's note. There were also copies of the money I'd given them — they were perfect replicas, except that they were colorless.

Great, I thought. *But I probably didn't need that anymore anyway.* I stooped down to gather the things, which all glowed brightly, since they all had been created brandnew. Bastille took the note, looked it over with a frown, then handed it to Kaz.

"So, your father really is down here somewhere," she said.

"Looks like it."

"And . . . the Curators claim he already gave up his soul."

I fell silent. *They gave back my papers when I asked,* I thought, *and they keep trying to get us to agree to give away our souls, but don't take them by force. They're bound by rules.*

I should have realized this earlier. You see, everything is bound by rules. Society has laws, as does nature, as do people. Many of society's rules have to do with expectations — which I'll talk about later — and therefore can be bent. A lot of nature's laws, however, are hard-set.

There are many more of these than you might expect. In fact, there are even natural laws relating to this book, my favorite of which is known as the Law of Pure Awesomeness. This law, of course, simply states that any book I write is awesome. I'm sorry, but it's a fact.

Who am I to argue with science?

"You," I said, looking toward a Curator. "Your kind have laws, don't they?"

The Curator paused. "Yes," it finally said. "Do you want to read them? I can give you a book that explains them in detail."

"No," I said. "No, I don't want to read about them. I want to hear about them. From you."

The Curator frowned.

"You have to tell me, don't you?" I said, smiling.

"It is my privilege to do so," the creature said. Then, it began to smile. "Of course, I am going to have to tell them to you in their original language."

"We are impressed that you speak ancient Greek," another said. "You are one who came to us prepared. There are few that do that, these days."

"But," another whispered, "we doubt that you know how to speak Elder Faxdarian."

Speak ancient Greek . . . , I thought, confused. Then it occurred to me. *They don't know about my Translator's Lenses! They think that because I understood them back at the beginning, I must have known the language.*

"Oh, I don't know about that," I said casually, swapping my Discerner's Lenses back for my Translator's Lenses. "Try me."

"Ha," one of them said in a very odd, strange language — it consisted mostly of spitting sounds. Like always, the Translator's Lenses let me hear the words in English. "The fool thinks he knows our language."

"Give him the rules, then," another hissed.

"First rule," said the one in front of me. "If anyone enters our domain bearing writing, we may separate them from their group and demand the writing be given to us. If they resist, we may take the writing, but we must return copies. We may hold these back for one hour but, unless the items are requested, can keep them from then on.

"Second rule, we may take the souls of those who enter, but we can do so only if the souls are offered freely and lawfully. Souls may be coerced, but not forced.

"Third rule, we may accept or reject a person's request for a soul contract. Once the contract is signed, we must provide the specific book requested, then refrain from taking their soul for the time specified in the contract. This time may not be longer than ten hours. If a person takes a book off its shelf without a contract, we may take their soul after ten seconds."

I shivered. Ten seconds or ten hours, it didn't seem to matter much. You still lost your soul. Of course, in my experience, there's really only one book in all of the world that is worth your soul to read — and you're holding it right now.

I accept credit cards.

"Fourth rule," the Curator continued. "We cannot directly harm those who enter."

Hence the traps, I thought. *Technically, when we trip those, we harm ourselves.* I continued to stare blankly ahead, acting as if I didn't understand a word they were saying.

"Fifth rule, when a person gives up their soul and becomes a Curator, we must deliver up their possessions to their kin, should a member of the family come to the Library and request such possessions.

"Sixth rule, and most important of them all. We are the protectors of knowledge and truth. We cannot lie, if asked a direct question."

The Curator fell silent.

"That it?" I asked.

If you've never seen a group of undead Curators with flaming eyes jump into the air with surprise . . . okay, I'm going to assume that you've never seen a group of undead Curators with flaming eyes jump into the air with surprise. Suffice it to say that the experience was quite amusing, in a creepy sort of way.

"He speaks our language!" one hissed.

"Impossible," another said. "Nobody outside the Library knows it."

"Could he be Tharandes?"

"He would have died millennia ago!"

Bastille and Kaz were watching me. I winked at them.

"Translator's Lenses," one of the Curators suddenly hissed. "See!"

"Impossible," another said. "Nobody could have gathered the Sands of Rashid."

"But he has . . . ," said a third. "Yes, they must be Lenses of Rashid!"

The three ghosts looked even more amazed than they had before.

"What's happening?" Bastille whispered.

"I'll tell you in a minute."

Based on the Curators' own rules, there was one way to discover if my father really had come to the Library of Alexandria and given up his soul. "I am the son of Attica Smedry," I said to the group of creatures. "I've come here for his personal effects. Your own laws say you must provide them to me."

There was a moment of silence.

"We cannot," one of the Curators finally said.

I sighed in relief. If my father had come to the Library, then he hadn't given up his soul. The Curators didn't have his personal items.

"We cannot," the Curator continued, skull teeth beginning to twist upward in an evil smile. "Because we have already given them away."

I felt a stab of shock. *No. It can't be!* "I don't believe you," I whispered.

"We cannot lie," another said. "Your father came to us, and he sold his soul to us. He only wanted three minutes to read the book, and then he was taken to become one of us.

His personal items have already been claimed — someone did so this very day."

"Who?" I demanded. "Who claimed them? My grandfather?"

"No," the Curator said, smile deepening. "They were claimed by Shasta Smedry. Your mother."

CHAPTER 12

I would like to apologize for the introduction to the last chapter. It occurs to me that this book, while random at times, really shouldn't waste its time on anarchist farm animals, whether or not they have bazookas. It's just plain silly, and since I abhor silliness, I would like to ask you to do me a favor.

Flip back two chapters, where the introduction should now contain the bunny paragraphs (since you cut them out of Chapter Eleven and pasted them in Chapter Ten instead). Cut those paragraphs out again, then go find a book by Jane Austen and paste them in there instead. The paragraphs will be much happier there, as Jane was quite fond of bunnies and bazookas, or so I'm told. It has to do with being a proper young lady living in the nineteenth century. But that's another story entirely.

I walked, head bowed, watching the ground in front of us for trip wires. I wore the Discerner's Lenses again, the Translator's Lenses stowed carefully in their pocket.

I was beginning to accept that my father — a man I'd never met, but whom I'd traveled halfway across the world to find — might be dead. Or worse than dead. If the Curators were telling the truth, Attica's soul had been ripped away from him, then used to fuel the creation of another twisted Curator of Alexandria. I would never know him, never meet him. My father was no more.

Equally disturbing was the knowledge that my mother was somewhere in these catacombs. Though I'd always known her as Ms. Fletcher, her actual name was Shasta. (Like many Librarians, she was named after a mountain.)

Ms. Fletcher — or Shasta, or whatever her name was — had worked as my personal caseworker during my years as a foster child in the Hushlands. She'd always treated me harshly, never giving me a hint that she was, in truth, my blood mother. Did she have something to do with the twisted, half-human Scrivener's Bone that was hunting me? How had she known about my father's trip to Alexandria? And what would she do if she found me here?

Something glowed on the ground in front of us, slightly brighter than the stones around it.

"Stop," I said, causing Bastille and Kaz to freeze. "Trip wire, right there."

Bastille knelt down. "So there is," she said, sounding impressed.

We carefully made our way over it, then continued on. During our last hour of walking, we'd left hallways filled with scrolls behind. More and more frequently, we were passing hallways filled with bookshelves. These books were still and musty, with cracking leather-bound covers, but they were obviously newer than the scrolls.

Every book ever written. Was there, somewhere in here, a room filled with paperback romance novels? The thought was amusing to me, but I wasn't sure why. The Curators claimed to collect knowledge. It didn't matter to them what kinds of stories or facts the books contained — they would gather it all, store it, and keep it safe. Until someone wanted to trade their soul for it.

I felt very sorry for the person who was tricked into giving up their soul for a trashy romance novel.

We kept moving. Theoretically, Kaz's Talent was leading us toward Australia, but it seemed to me like we were just walking aimlessly. Considering the nature of his Talent, that was probably a good sign.

"Kaz," I said. "Did you know my mother?"

The short man eyed me. "Sure did. She was . . . well, is . . . my sister-in-law."

"They never divorced?"

Kaz shook his head. "I'm not sure what happened — they had a falling-out, obviously. Your father gave you away to be cared for in foster homes, and your mother took up position watching over you." He paused, then shook his head. "We were all there at your naming, Al. That was the day when your father pronounced the Sands of Rashid upon you as your inheritance. We're still not sure how he got them to you at the right time, in the right place."

"Oracle's Lenses," I said.

"He has a pair of *those*?"

I nodded.

"Walnuts! The prophets in Ventat are supposed to have the only pair in existence. I wonder where Attica found some."

I shrugged. "He mentioned them in the letter he sent me."

Kaz nodded thoughtfully. "Well, your father disappeared just a few days after pronouncing your blessing, so I guess there just wasn't time for a divorce. Your mother could ask for one, but she really has no motivation to do so. After all, she'd lose her Talent."

"*What?*"

"Her Talent, Al," Kaz said. "She's a Smedry now."

"Only by marriage."

"Doesn't matter," Kaz said. "The spouse of a Smedry gains their husband's or wife's same Talent as soon as the marriage is official."

I'd assumed that Talents were genetic — that they were passed on from parents to children, kind of the same way that skin color or hair color was. But this meant they were something different. That seemed important.

That does make some things make more sense, I thought. *Grandpa Smedry said he'd worried that my mother had only married my father for his Talent.* I'd assumed that she'd been enthralled with the Talent, much as someone might marry a rock star for his guitar skillz. However, that didn't sound like my mother.

She'd wanted a Talent. "So, my mother's Talent is . . ."

"Losing things," Kaz said. "Just like your father's." He smiled, eyes twinkling. "I don't think she's ever figured out how to use it properly. She's a Librarian — she believes in order, lists, and catalogues. To use a Talent, you just have to be able to let yourself be out of control for a while."

I nodded. "What did you think? When he married her, I mean."

"I thought he was an idiot," Kaz said. "And I told him so, as is the solemn duty of younger brothers. He married her anyway, the stubborn hazelnut."

About what I expected, I thought.

"But, Attica seemed to love her," Kaz continued with a sigh. "And, to be perfectly honest, she wasn't as bad as many Librarians. For a while, it seemed like they might actually make things work. Then . . . it fell apart. Right around the time you were born."

I frowned. "But, she was a Librarian agent all along, right? She just wanted to get Father's Talent."

"Some still think that's the case. She really did seem to care for him, though. I . . . well, I just don't know."

"She *had* to be faking," I said stubbornly.

"If you say so," Kaz said. "I think you may be letting your preconceptions cloud your thinking."

I shook my head. "No. I don't do that."

"Oh, you don't?" Kaz said, amused. "Well then, let's try something. Why don't you tell me about your grandfather; pretend I don't know anything about him, and you want to describe him to me."

"Okay," I said slowly. "Grandpa Smedry is a brilliant Oculator who is a little bit zany, but who is one of the Free Kingdom's most important figures. He has the Talent to arrive late to things."

"Great," Kaz said. "Now tell me about Bastille."

I eyed her, and she shot me a threatening glance. "Uh, Bastille is a Crystin. I think that's about all I can say without her throwing something at me."

"Good enough. Australia?"

I shrugged. "She seems a bit scatterbrained, but is a good person. She's an Oculator and has a Smedry Talent."

"Okay," Kaz said. "Now talk about me."

"Well, you're a short person who —"

"Stop," Kaz said.

I did so, shooting him a questioning glance.

"Why is it," Kaz said, "that with the others, the first thing you described about them was their job or their personality? Yet, with me, the first thing you mentioned was my height?"

"I . . . uh . . ."

Kaz laughed. "I'm not trying to trap you, kid. But, maybe you see why I get so annoyed sometimes. The trouble with being different is that people start defining you by *what* you are instead of by *who* you are."

I fell silent.

"Your mother is a Librarian," Kaz said. "Because of that, we tend to think of her as a Librarian first, and a person second. Our knowledge of her as a Librarian clouds everything else."

"She's not a good person, Kaz," I said. "She offered to sell me to a Dark Oculator."

"Did she?" Kaz asked. "What exactly did she say?"

I thought back to the time when Bastille, Sing, and I had been hiding in the library, listening to Ms. Fletcher speak with Blackburn. "Actually," I said, "she didn't say anything. It was the Dark Oculator who said something like, 'You'd sell the boy too, wouldn't you? You impress me.' And she just shrugged or nodded or something."

"So," Kaz said, "she *didn't* offer to sell you out."

"She didn't contradict Blackburn."

Kaz shook his head. "Shasta has her own agenda, kid. I don't think any of us can presume to understand exactly what she's up to. Your father saw something in her. I still think he's a fool for marrying her, but for a Librarian, she wasn't too bad."

I wasn't convinced. My bias against Librarians wasn't the *only* thing making me distrust Shasta. She had consistently berated me as a child, saying I was worthless. (I now know she had been trying to get me to stop using my Talent, for fear it would expose me to those who were searching for the Sands.) Either way, she'd been my mother all that time, and she hadn't ever given me even a hint of confirmation.

Though . . . she *had* stayed with me, always, watching over me.

I pushed that thought aside. She didn't deserve credit for that — she'd just been hoping for the chance to grab the Sands of Rashid. The very day they arrived, she showed up and swiped them.

". . . don't know, Kaz," Bastille was saying. "*I* think that the main reason people think of your height first is because of that ridiculous List of yours."

"My List is *not* ridiculous," Kaz said with a huff. "It's very scientific."

"Oh?" Bastille asked. "Didn't you claim that 'short people are better because it takes them longer to walk places, therefore they get more exercise'?"

"That one has been clinically proven," Kaz said, pointing at her.

"It does seem a bit of a stretch," I said, smiling.

"You forget Reason number one," he said. "'Don't argue with the short person.' He's always right."

Bastille snorted. "It's a good thing you don't claim short people are more humble."

Kaz fell silent. "That's Reason two thirty-six," he muttered quietly. "I just haven't mentioned that one yet."

Bastille shot me a glance through her sunglasses, and I could tell she was rolling her eyes. However, even though I didn't believe Kaz about my mother, I thought his comments about how to treat people were valid.

Who we are — meaning, the person we become by doing things — which — incidentally — is actually a function of who we are — for example, I've become an Oculator — which is quite fun — by doing things that relate to Oculators — not who we can be — is more important — actually — than what we look like.

For instance, the fact that I use lots of dashes in my writing is part of what makes me, me. I'd rather be known by this — since it's cool — than by the fact that I have a big nose. Which I don't. Why are you looking at me like that?

"Wait!" I said, holding out a hand.

Bastille froze.

"Trip wire," I said, heart pounding. Her foot hovered just a few inches from it.

She backed away, and Kaz squatted down. "Well done, kid. It's a good thing you have those Lenses."

"Yeah," I said, taking them off and cleaning them. "I guess." I still wished I had a weapon instead of another pair of Lenses that showed me random stuff. Wouldn't a sword have been equally useful?

Of course, I might think that just because I really like swords. Give me the chance, and I'd probably cut my wedding cake with one.

I did have to admit, though, that I'd made pretty good use of the Discerner's Lenses. Maybe I'd discounted them too quickly at first. I cleaned my Lenses, feeling an odd sensation from inside. It was slight, a little like indigestion, but less foody.

I shook my head and put the Discerner's Lenses back on, then guided the other two over the trip wire. As I did, I noticed something interesting. "There's a second trip wire just a few feet ahead."

"They're getting more clever," Bastille said. "They figured we'd see this one, but hoped we'd feel safe once we passed it — then go right on and trip the second."

I nodded, glancing at the Curators floating behind. I noticed that the odd sensation was getting stronger. It was hard to explain. It wasn't really a sick feeling. More like a slight itch on my emotions.

"We need to find Australia quickly, Kaz," Bastille said. "Is it supposed to take this long?"

"Never can tell, with the Talent," Kaz said. "Australia might not actually be lost. If that's the case, it will take me a lot longer to find her than it took me to find you. Like I mentioned earlier, if I don't know where to go, then my Talent can't really take me there."

Bastille didn't seem pleased to hear this. "Maybe we should start looking for the Old Smedry instead."

"If I know my father, he's not lost," Kaz said, rubbing his chin. "He'll be even more difficult to find."

I was barely paying attention to them. The itch was still there. It wasn't the same feeling that I got from the hunter that was chasing me, but it was similar. . . .

"So, do we just keep going?" Bastille asked.

"I guess so," Kaz said.

"No," I said suddenly, looking at them. "Kaz, turn off your Talent."

Bastille looked at me, frowning. "What is it?"

"Someone's using a Lens nearby."

"The Scrivener's Bone chasing us?"

I shook my head. "This is a regular Lens, not a twisted one like he uses. It means there is an Oculator close to us." I paused, then pointed. "That way."

Bastille shared a look with Kaz. "Let's go check it out," she said.

CHAPTER 13

I have to apologize for the introduction to that last chapter. It was far too apologetic. There's been too much apologizing going on in this book. I'm sorry. I want to prove to you that I'm a liar, not a wimp.

The thing is, you never know who is going to be reading your books. I've tried to write this one for members of both the Hushlands and the Free Kingdoms, and that's tough enough. However, even within the Hushlands, the variety of people who could pick this book up is incredible.

You could be a young boy, wanting to read an adventure story. You could be a young girl, wanting to investigate the truth of the Librarian Conspiracy. You might be a mother, reading this book because you've heard that so many of your kids are reading it. Or you could be a serial killer who specializes in reading books, then seeking out the authors and murdering them in horrible ways.

(If you happen to fall into that last category, you should know that my name isn't really Alcatraz Smedry, nor is it Brandon Sanderson. My name is really Garth Nix, and you can find me in Australia. Oh, and I insulted your mother once. What're you going to do about it, huh?)

Anyway, it's very difficult to relate this story to everyone who might be reading my book. So, I've decided not to try. Instead, I'll just say something that makes no sense to anyone: Flagwat the happy beansprout.

Confusion, after all, is the *true* universal language.

"The feeling is coming from that direction," I said, pointing. Unfortunately, "that direction" happened to be straight through a wall full of books.

"So . . . one of the books is an Oculator?" Kaz asked.

I rolled my eyes.

He chuckled. "I understood what you meant. Stop acting like Bastille. Obviously, we have to find a way around. There must be another hallway on the other side."

I nodded, but . . . the Lens felt *close.* We'd walked down a few rows already, coming to this point, and I felt like it was just on the other side of the wall.

I took off my Discerner's Lenses, putting on my Oculator's Lenses instead. One of their main functions was to reveal Oculatory power, and they made the entire wall glow with a bright white light. I stumbled back, shocked by the powerful illumination.

"Glowing, eh?" Bastille asked, walking up to me.

I nodded.

"That's strange," she said. "It takes time for an area to charge with Oculatory power. The Lens you sensed must have been here for a while if it has started making things around it glow."

"What are you implying?" I asked.

She shook her head. "I'm not sure. When you first spoke, I assumed we were close to Grandpa Smedry, since he's the only other Oculator we know to be down here. Except for, well, your father, and he . . ."

I didn't want to think about that. "It's probably not Grandpa. He came down here only a little while before we did."

"What, then?" Bastille asked.

I took off my Oculator's Lenses, then put on my Discerner's Lenses again. I walked carefully along the wall full of books, inspecting the brickwork.

I didn't have to look far before I discovered that one section of the wall was much older than all of the others.

"Something *is* back there," I said. "I think there might be a secret passage or something."

"How do we trigger it?" Bastille asked. "Pull one of the books?"

"I guess."

One of the ever-present Curators floated closer. "Yes," it said. "Pull one of the books. Take it."

I paused, hand halfway up to the shelf. "I'm not going to take it; I'll just shake it a bit."

"Try it," the Curator whispered. "Whether you pick up a book, or whether it falls off accidentally, it does not matter. Move even one of the books a few inches off its shelf, and your soul is ours."

I lowered my hand. The Curator seemed too eager to scare me away from trying to move one of the books. *It seems like they don't want me to find out what is behind there.*

I inspected the bookshelf. There was enough space to the side of it — between it and the next bookshelf over — that I could reach through and touch the back wall. I took a deep breath, leaning up against the bookcase, careful to keep from touching any of the books.

"Alcatraz . . . ," Bastille said with concern.

I nodded, careful as I pressed my hand against the back wall. *If I break this, and the bookshelf falls over, it will cost me my soul.*

My Discerner's Lenses told me that this portion of the brick wall behind the bookshelf was older than even the rest of the walls and floor. Whatever was behind that wall had been there even before the Curators moved into the area.

I released my power.

The wall crumbled, bricks breaking free of their mortar. I anxiously tried to hold the bookcase steady as the wall collapsed behind it. Kaz rushed forward, grabbing it on the other side, and Bastille pressed her hands against the books that were teetering slightly on their shelves. Apparently, none of this was enough to give the Curators leave to take our souls, because they watched with an air of petulance as not a single book slid out.

I wiped my brow. The entire wall had fallen away, and there *was* some kind of room back there.

"That was rash, Alcatraz," Bastille said, folding her arms.

"He's a true Smedry!" Kaz said, laughing.

I glanced at the two of them, suddenly embarrassed. "Someone had to break down that wall. It's the only way we were going to get through."

Bastille shrugged. "You complain about having to make decisions, then you make one like that without even asking. Do you want to be in charge or not?"

"Uh . . . Well . . . I, that is . . ."

"Brilliant," she said, peeking into the hole between the bookcases. "Very inspiring. Kaz, do you think we can get through?"

Kaz was prying a lamp off the wall. "Sure we can. Though we may have to move that bookcase."

Bastille eyed it and then, sighing, helped me ease the bookcase back from the wall just a few inches. We didn't, fortunately, lose any books — or any souls — in the process. Once finished, Kaz was able to slip through the opening.

"Wow!" he said.

Bastille, standing on that side of the bookcase, went next. I, therefore, had to go last — which I found rather unfair, considering that I'd been the one to discover the place. However, all feelings of annoyance vanished as I stepped into the chamber.

It was a tomb.

I'd seen enough movies about wisecracking archaeologists to know what an Egyptian pharaoh's tomb looked like. A massive sarcophagus sat in the center, and there were delicate golden pillars spaced around it. Mounds of wealth were heaped in the corners — coins, lamps, statues of animals. The floor itself seemed to be of pure gold.

So, I did what anyone would do if he'd discovered an ancient Egyptian tomb. I yelped for joy, then rushed directly over to the nearest pile of gold and reached for a handful.

"Alcatraz, wait!" Bastille said, grabbing my arm with a burst of Crystin speed.

"What?" I asked in annoyance. "You're not going to give me some kind of nonsense about grave robbing or curses, are you?"

"Shattering Glass, no," Bastille said. "But look — those coins have words on them."

I glanced to the side and noticed that she was right. Each coin was stamped with a foreign kind of character that wasn't Egyptian, as far as I could tell. "So?" I asked. "What does it matter if . . ."

I trailed off, then glanced at the three Curators, who floated in through the wall in a fittingly ghostly manner.

"Curators," I said. "Do these coins count as books?"

"They are written," one said. "Paper, cloth, or metal, it matters not."

"You can check one out, if you wish," another whispered, floating up to me.

I shivered, then glanced at Bastille. "You just saved my life," I said, feeling numb.

She shrugged. "I'm a Crystin. That's what we do." However, she did seem to walk a little bit more confidently as she joined Kaz, who was inspecting the sarcophagus.

You should have realized that I wouldn't be able to have any of the coins. That's what happens in stories like this. Characters in books find heaps of gold or hidden treasure all over the place — but then, of course, they never get to spend a penny of it. Instead, they either

  1) Lose it in an earthquake or natural disaster.

  II) Put it in a backpack that then breaks at a climactic moment, dropping all of the treasure as the heroes flee.

  C) Use it to rescue their orphanage from foreclosure.

206

Stupid orphanages.

Anyway, it is very common for authors to do things like this to the people in their stories. Why? Well, we will *claim* it's because we want to teach the reader that the real wealth is friendship, or caring, or something stupid like that. In reality, we're just mean people. We like to torment our readers, and that translates to tormenting our characters. After all, there is only one thing more frustrating than finding a pile of gold, then having it snatched away from you.

And that's being told that at least you learned something from the experience.

I sighed, leaving the coins behind.

"Oh, don't mope, Alcatraz," Bastille said, waving indifferently toward another corner of the room. "Just take some of those gold bars instead. They don't seem to have anything written on them."

I turned and smacked my forehead, suddenly realizing that I *wasn't* in a fictional story. This was an autobiography and was completely real — which meant that the "lesson" I could learn from it all is that grave robbing is way cool.

"Good idea!" I said. "Curators, do those bars count as books?"

The ghosts floated sullenly, one shooting an angry glare at Bastille. "No," it finally said.

I smiled, then proceeded to stuff a few bars in my pocket, then a few more in Bastille's pack. In case you were wondering, yes. Gold really is as heavy as they say. And it's totally worth carrying anyway.

"Don't you guys want any of this?" I asked, putting another bar in my jacket pocket.

Kaz shrugged. "You and I are Smedries, Alcatraz. We're friends to kings, counselors to emperors, defenders of the Free Kingdoms. Our family is incredibly wealthy, and we can pretty much have anything we want. I mean, that silimatic dragon we crashed was probably worth more money than most people would ever be able to spend in a lifetime."

"Oh," I said.

"And I kind of took a vow of poverty," Bastille said, grimacing.

That was new. "Really?"

She nodded. "If I brought some of that gold, it would just end up going to the Knights of Crystallia — and I'm a little annoyed with them right now."

I stuffed a few bars in my pocket for her anyway.

"Alcatraz, come look at this," Kaz said.

I reluctantly left the rest of the gold behind, clinking my way over to the other two. They stood a distance away from the sarcophagus, not approaching. "What's wrong?"

"Look closely," Kaz said, pointing.

I did, squinting in the light of the single lamp. With effort, I saw what he was talking about. Dust. Hanging in the air, motionless.

"What's that?" I asked.

"I don't know," Kaz said. "But, if you look, there's a bubble of clean ground around the sarcophagus. No dust."

There was a large circle on the ground, running around the casket, where either the dust had been cleaned away, or it had never fallen. Now that I thought to notice, I realized that the rest of this room was far more dusty than the Library. It hadn't been disturbed in some time.

"There's something odd about this place," Bastille said, hands on hips.

"Yeah," I said, frowning. "Those hieroglyphics don't quite look like any I've seen before."

"Seen a lot?" she asked, raising a skeptical eyebrow.

I flushed. "I mean, they don't look the way Egyptian ones should."

It was hard to explain. As one might expect, the walls were covered with small pictures, drawn as if to be words. Yet, instead of people with cattle or eagle heads, there were pictures of dragons and serpents. Instead of scarabs, there were odd geometric shapes, like runes. Above the doorway where we had come in, there was . . .

"Kaz!" I said, pointing.

He turned, then his eyes opened wide. There, inscribed over the door, was a circle split into four sections, with symbols written in each of the four pieces. Just like the diagram Kaz had drawn for me on the ground, the one about the different kinds of Talents. The Incarnate Wheel.

This one also had a small circle in the center with its own symbol, along with a ring around the outside, split into two sections, each with another character in them.

"It could just be a coincidence," Kaz said slowly. "I mean, it's just a circle split into four pieces. It isn't *necessarily* the same diagram."

"It is," I said. "It feels right."

"Well, maybe the Curators put it there," Kaz said. "They saw me draw it on the ground, and copied it down. Maybe they have placed it here for us to find, so it would confuse us."

I shook my head. "I've still got my Discerner's Lenses on. That inscription is as old as the rest of the tomb."

"What does it say?" Bastille asked. "Won't that tell us what it is?"

Why didn't I think of that? I thought, embarrassed again. Bastille certainly was quick on her feet. Or maybe I was slow. Let's not discuss that possibility any further. Forget I mentioned it.

"Can I read that text without losing my soul?" I asked.

We looked at the Curators. One reluctantly spoke. "You can," it said. "You lose your soul when you check out or move a book. A symbol on the wall can be read without being checked out."

It made sense. If it were that easy to get souls, the Curators could just have posted signs, then taken the souls of any who read them.

With that, I pulled off my Discerner's Lenses and put on my Translator's Lenses. They immediately interpreted the strange symbols.

"The inner squares say the things you taught, Kaz," I said. "Time, Space, Matter, Knowledge."

Kaz whistled. "Walnuts! That means whoever built this place knew an awful lot about Smedry Talents and arcane theory. What about that symbol in the middle of the circle? What does it say?"

"It says Breaking," I said quietly.

My Talent.

"Interesting," Kaz said. "They give it its own circle on the diagram. What is that outer circle?"

The ring was split into two pieces. "One says Identity," I said. "The other says Possibility."

Kaz looked thoughtful. "Classical philosophy," he said. "Metaphysics. It appears that our dead friend there was a philosopher of some kind. Makes sense, considering that we're near Alexandria."

I wasn't paying much attention to that. Instead, I turned, hesitant, to read the words on the walls. My Translator's Lenses instantly changed them to English for me.

I immediately wished that I hadn't read them.

CHAPTER 14

Time for a history lesson.

Stop complaining. This isn't an adventure story; it's a factual autobiography. The purpose isn't to entertain you, but to teach you. If you want to be entertained, go to school and listen to the imaginary facts your teachers make up.

The Incarna. I talked about them in my last book, I believe. They're the ones who developed the Forgotten Language. In the Free Kingdoms, everyone is a little annoyed at them. After all, the Incarna supposedly had this fantastic understanding of both technology and magic. But, instead of sharing their wisdom with the rest of the world, they developed the Forgotten Language and then — somehow — managed to change all of their texts and writings so that they were written in this language.

No, the Forgotten Language *wasn't* their original method of writing. Everybody knows that. They *transformed* all of their books into it. Kind of like . . . applying an encrypting program to a computer document. Except, it affected all forms of writing, whether on paper, in metal, or in stone.

Nobody knows how they managed this. They were a race of mega-evolved, highly intelligent superbeings. I doubt it was all that tough for them. They could probably turn lead into gold, grant immortality, and make a mean dish of cold fusion too. Doesn't really matter. Nobody can read what they left behind.

Except me. With my Translator's Lenses.

Perhaps now you can see why the Librarians would hire a twisted, half-human assassin to hunt me down and retrieve them, eh?

"Alcatraz?" Bastille said, apparently noticing how white my face had become. "What's wrong?"

I stared at the wall with its strange words, trying to sort through what I was reading. She shook my arm.

"Alcatraz?" she asked again, then glanced at the wall. "What does it say?"

I read the words again.

Beware all ye who visit this place of rest. Know that The Dark Talent has been released upon the world. We have failed to keep it contained.

Our desires have brought us low. We sought to touch the powers of eternity, then draw them down upon ourselves. But we brought with them something we did not intend.

Be careful of it. Guard it well, and beware its use. Do not rely upon it. We have seen the possibilities of the future and the ultimate end. It could destroy so much, if given the chance.

The Bane of Incarna. That which twists, that which corrupts, and that which destroys. The Dark Talent.

The Talent of Breaking.

"This place is important," I whispered. "This place is really, *really* important."

"Why?" Bastille said. "Shattering Glass, Smedry. When are you going to tell me what that says?"

"Get out your pen and paper," I said, kneeling. "I need to write this down."

Bastille sighed, but did as I asked, fetching a pen and paper from her pack. Kaz wandered over, watching with interest as I transcribed the writing on the wall.

"What language is that, anyway?" I asked. "It mentions the Incarna, but it's not the Forgotten Language."

"That's old Nalhallan," Kaz said. "I can't read it, but we have a few scholars back in the capital who can. When the Incarna fell, its few survivors ended up in Nalhalla to live."

I finished the translation. Then, immediately, the three Curators surrounded me.

"You must give up all writings to the Library when you enter," one hissed. "A copy will be returned to you once we have completed it. If a copy cannot be made in one hour's time, we will return the original instead."

I rolled my eyes. "Oh, for heaven's sake!" However, I let them pull the sheet away and vanish with it.

Bastille was frowning — she'd read the translation as I wrote it. "That inscription makes it seem like your Talent is dangerous."

"It is," I said. "Do you know how many times I've nearly been beaten up for breaking something at the wrong time?"

"But —" She cut off, however, obviously sensing that I didn't want to talk about it further.

To be honest, I didn't know what to think. It was strange enough to find ancient writings that dealt with Smedry Talents. To have them give a caution about mine specifically . . . well, it was a little disturbing.

That was the first time I really got any hint of the troubles that were coming. You Free Kingdomers call me a savior. Can I really be considered a savior if I *caused* the very problem I helped fix?

"Wait a moment," Bastille said. "Didn't we get drawn here by an Oculatory Lens? Whatever happened to that?"

"That's right," I said, standing. I could still sense it working, though I'd been distracted by everything else in the tomb.

I swapped my Translator's Lenses for my Oculator's Lenses, then had to turn down their power because of how blinding the room was. Once I'd done so, I could see the Lens that had drawn me here. It was set into the lid of the sarcophagus.

"It's there," I said, pointing. "On the top of the sar-cophagus."

"I don't trust that thing," Kaz said. "That circle around it is strange. We should leave, gather a research team, then come back and study this place in detail."

I nodded absently. Then, I walked toward the sar-cophagus.

"Alcatraz!" Bastille said. "Are you going to do something stupid and brash again?"

I turned. "Yeah."

She blinked. "Oh. Well, then, you probably shouldn't. Consider me opposed to it. Whatever it is."

"Objection noted," I said.

"I —" Bastille said. She stopped as I stepped into the circle of clean ground around the sarcophagus.

Everything immediately changed. Dust began to fall around me, sparkling like very fine powdered metal. Lamps burned with bright flames set to the top of the pillars around the sarcophagus. It was like I'd entered a small column of golden light. Somehow, I'd moved from a long-dead tomb to someplace alive with motion.

There was still a sense of reverence to the area. I turned, noticing Bastille and Kaz standing outside the ring of light. They seemed frozen in place, mouths open as if to speak.

I turned back to the sarcophagus, the dust falling very faintly in the air, sprinkling over everything. I held up a hand. It was indeed metallic, and it glittered with a yellow sheen. Gold dust.

Why had I stepped blindly into the circle like that?

It's hard to explain. Imagine you have the hiccups. In fact, you not only have the hiccups, you have *The* Hiccups. These are the hiccups to end all hiccups. You've hiccupped all of your life, without a moment of freedom. You've hiccupped so much that you've lost friends, made everyone annoyed at you, and grown pretty down on yourself.

And then, amazingly, you discover a group of people who have similar problems. Some of them burp all the time, others sniffle all the time, and still others have really bad gas. They all make annoying noises, but they come from a land where that's really cool. They're all impressed with your hiccupping.

You hang out with these people for a time, and start to grow proud of your hiccups. Then, you pass a billboard that mentions — for the first time — that your hiccups will probably end up destroying the world.

You might, then, feel a little like I did. Confused, betrayed, unsettled. Willing to step into a strange ring of power to confront, hopefully, the person who made the billboard.

Even if he did happen to be dead.

I pushed aside the top of the sarcophagus. It was heavier than I'd expected, and I had to heave. It clattered to the floor, scattering gold dust.

There was a man's body inside, and he wasn't even a bit decomposed. In fact, he looked so lifelike that I jumped backward.

The man in the sarcophagus didn't move. I edged closer, eyeing him. He looked to be in his fifties, and was wearing an ancient set of clothing — a kind of skirtlike wrap around the lower legs, then a flowing cloaklike shirt on his back that left his bare chest exposed. He had a golden headband around his forehead.

I hesitantly poked his face. (Don't pretend you wouldn't have done the same.)

The man didn't move. So, carefully, cringing, I checked for a pulse. Nothing.

I stepped back. Now, perhaps you've seen a dead body before. I sincerely hope that you haven't, but let's be realistic. People die sometimes. They have to — if they didn't, funeral homes and graveyards would go out of business.

Dead bodies don't look like they were ever alive. Corpses tend to look like they're made from wax — they don't seem like people at all, but mannequins.

This body didn't look that way. The cheeks were still flush, the face surreal in the way it seemed ready to take a breath at any moment.

I glanced back at Bastille and Kaz. They were still frozen, as if time weren't moving for them. I looked back at the body, and suddenly began to catch a hint of what might be going on.

I put on my Translator's Lenses, then walked over to the discarded lid of the sarcophagus. There, printed in ornate letters, was a name:

Allekatrase the Lens-wielder, first Bearer of the Dark Talent.

Intrinsically, my Translator's Lenses let me know that the word *Lens-wielder* when spoken in ancient Nalhallan would sound different to my ears. The ancient Nalhallan word for "Lens" was *smaed* and their word for "person who uses" was *dary*.

Allekatrase the Lens-wielder. Allekatrase Smaed-dary.

Alcatraz Smedry the First.

Golden dust fell around me, sprinkling my hair. "You broke time, didn't you?" I asked. "Kaz mentioned that there were legends of you having done so. You created for yourself a tomb where time would not pass, where you could rest without decomposing."

It was the ultimate method of embalming. I personally suspect that the Egyptian custom of making mummies of their kings came from the story of Alcatraz Smedry the First.

"I have your Talent," I said, stepping up beside the sarcophagus, looking at the man inside. "What am I supposed to do with it? Can I control it? Or will it always control me?"

The body was silent. They're like that. Completely lacking in social graces, those corpses.

"Did it destroy you?" I asked. "Is that what the warning is for?"

The body was so serene. Gold dust was beginning to gather on its face. Finally, I just sighed, kneeling down to look at the Lens in the lid of the sarcophagus. It was completely clear, with no color to indicate what it did. Yet, I knew it was powerful because it had drawn me here.

I reached out and tried to pry it free. It was stuck on the lid very soundly, but I wasn't about to leave a Lens that powerful sitting in a forgotten tomb.

I touched the lid and released my Talent into it. Immediately, the Lens popped free, flipping up into the air. I was caught so off guard that I barely managed to grab it before it fell and shattered.

As soon as I touched the Lens, it stopped giving off power. The bubble of strange time-shift continued to be in force, however, so the Lens hadn't been behind that.

I moved to stand up, but then noticed something. In the place where the Lens had been affixed, there was an inscription. It would have been hidden beneath the glass of the Lens, which had a small black paper backing to keep the text from being seen until the Lens was removed.

It was in ancient Nalhallan. With my Translator's Lenses, I could read it with ease.

To my descendant, the tiny inscription read.

> If you have released this Lens, then I know you have the Dark Talent. Part of me rejoices, for this means it is still being protected and borne by our family, as is our curse.
>
> Yet, I am also worried, for it means you haven't found a way to banish it. As long as the corrupting Talent remains, it is a danger.
>
> This Lens is the most precious of my collection. I have given others to my son. His lesser Talent, though corrupted, is not to be feared. Only when the Talent can Break is it dangerous. In all others, it simply taints what they have.
>
> Use the Lens. Pass on this knowledge, if it has been forgotten.
>
> And care well for the burden, blessing, and curse you have been given.

I sat back, trying to decide what I thought of the words. I wished that I had something I could write with, but then decided that it was better that I didn't copy the text. The Curators would take what I wrote, and if they didn't already know of the inscription, I didn't want them to.

I stood up. With some effort, I managed to get the lid of the sarcophagus back on. Then, I lay my hand on the inscription and somehow Broke it. The text of the letters scrambled, becoming gibberish, even to my Translator's Lenses.

I pulled my hand back, surprised. I'd never done anything like that before. I stood silently, then solemnly bowed my head to the sarcophagus, which had been carved to match the face of the man who rested inside.

"I'll do my best," I said. Then I stepped from the circle.

The light faded. The room became musty and old again, and Bastille and Kaz began moving.

"— don't think this is a good idea," Bastille said.

"Objection noted again," I said, dusting the gold powder from my shoulders, where it had gathered like King Midas's dandruff.

"Alcatraz?" Kaz asked. "What just happened?"

"Time moves differently in there," I said, looking back at the sarcophagus. It seemed unchanged, the dust hanging in the air, the lamps extinguished. The Lens on the lid, however, was gone. I still had it in my hand.

"I think stepping into that circle takes you back in time to the moment he died," I said. "Something like that. I'm not exactly sure."

"That's . . . very odd," Kaz said. "Did you find out who he was?"

I nodded, looking down at the Lens. "Alcatraz the First."

The other two were silent.

"That's impossible, Al," Kaz said. "I've *seen* the tomb of Alcatraz the First. It's down in the Nalhallan royal catacombs. It's one of the city's greatest tourist attractions."

"It's a fake," Bastille said.

We both looked at her sharply.

"The royal family made it a thousand years back or so," she said, glancing away. "As a symbol of Nalhalla's founding. It bothered the royals that they didn't know where Alcatraz the First was buried, so they came up with a fake historical site to commemorate him."

Kaz whistled softly. "I guess you'd know, Bastille. That's some cover-up. But, why is he here, in the Library of Alexandria, of all places?"

"This room is older than the parts around it," I said. "I'd say that the Curators moved their Library here on purpose. Weren't you the one who told me that it changed locations in favor of a place with more room?"

"True," Kaz said. "What's that Lens?"

I held it up. "I'm not sure; I found it on the sarcophagus. Bastille, do you recognize it?"

She shook her head. "It's not tinted. It could do anything."

"Maybe I should just activate it."

Bastille shrugged, and Kaz seemed to have no objections. So, hesitantly, I tried it. Nothing happened. I looked through the Lens, but couldn't see anything different about the room.

"Nothing?" Bastille asked.

I shook my head, frowning. *He called this his most powerful of Lenses. So, what does it do?*

"It makes sense, I guess," Kaz said. "It was active before — it's what drew you here. Maybe all it does is send out a signal to other Oculators."

"Maybe," I said, unconvinced. I slipped it into the single-Lens pocket in my jacket that had once held my Firebringer's Lens.

"We should probably just show it to my father," Kaz said. "He'll be able to . . ."

He kept talking, but I stopped paying attention. Bastille was acting oddly. She'd suddenly perked up, growing tense. She glanced out the broken wall.

"Bastille?" I asked, cutting Kaz off.

"Shattering Glass!" she said, then took off in a dash out of the room.

Kaz and I stood, dumbfounded.

"What do we do?" Kaz asked.

"Follow her!" I said, slipping out of the room — careful not to tip over the bookcase outside. Kaz followed, grabbing Bastille's pack and pulling out a pair of Warrior's Lenses. As I took off at a dash down the hallway after Bastille, he managed to keep up by virtue of the enhancements the Lenses granted.

I quickly began to realize why characters in books tend to lose their gold before the end of the story. That stuff was *heavy*. Reluctantly, I tossed most of the gold to the side, keeping only a couple of bars in my pocket.

Even without the gold, however, neither of us was fast enough to follow a Crystin.

"Bastille!" I yelled, watching her disappear into the distance.

There was no response. Soon, Kaz and I reached an intersection and paused, puffing. We'd moved into yet another part of the Library. Here, instead of rows of scrolls or bookcases, we were in a section that looked like a dungeon. There were lots of intermixing hallways and small rooms, lamps flickering softly on the walls.

To make things more confusing, some of the doorways — even some of the hallways — had bars set across them, blocking the way forward. My suspicion is that this part of the Library was intended to be a maze — another means of frustrating people.

Bastille suddenly rushed back toward us, running out of a side corridor.

"Bastille?" I asked.

She cursed and passed us, going down another of the side hallways. I glanced at Kaz, who just shrugged. So, we took off after her again.

As we ran, I noticed something. A feeling. I froze, causing Kaz to pull up short beside me.

"What?" he asked.

"He's near," I said.

"Who?"

"The hunter. The one chasing us."

"National Union of Teachers!" Kaz swore. "You're sure?"

I nodded. Ahead, I could hear Bastille yelling. We moved, passing a set of bars on our right. Through them, I could see another hallway. It would be very easy to get lost in this section of the Library.

But, then, we were already lost. So, it didn't really seem to matter. Bastille came running back, and this time I managed to grab her arm as she ran by. She jerked to a halt, brow sweating, looking wild-eyed.

"Bastille!" I said. "What is going on?"

"My mother," Bastille said. "She's near, and she's in pain. I can't get to her because every one of these shattering passages is a dead end!"

Draulin? I thought. *Here?* I opened my mouth to ask how Bastille could possibly know that, and then I felt something. That dark, oppressive force. The twisted, unnatural feeling given off by a Lens that had been forged with Oculator blood. It was near. Very near.

I looked down a side hallway. Lamps flickered along its

sides, and at the very end, I saw a massive iron grate covering the way forward.

Beyond the grate stood a shadowed figure, one arm unnaturally long, the face misshapen.

And it held Draulin's Crystin sword in its hands.

CHAPTER 15

It's my fault.

I'll admit the truth; I did it. You've undoubtedly noticed it by now, if you've been reading closely. I apologize. Of all the dirty tricks I've used, this is undoubtedly the nastiest of them all. I realize it might have ruined the book for you up until now, but I couldn't help myself.

You see, doing something like this consistently, over fourteen chapters, was quite challenging. And I'm always up for a challenge. When you noticed it, you probably realized how clever I was, even as you blushed. I know this is supposed to be a book for kids, and I thought it was well enough hidden that it wouldn't come out. I guess I was too obvious.

I'd have taken it out, but it's just so clever. Most people won't be able to find it, even though it's there in every

231

chapter, on every page. The most brilliant literary joke I've ever made.

My apologies.

I stood, facing down the silhouetted creature, still holding on to Bastille's arm. I slowly came to understand something.

I had been wrong to run from the creature — that had caused my group to get split up. Now the hunter could take us one at a time, grabbing us from the catacombs as we ran about in confusion.

We couldn't continue to run. It was time to confront it. I gulped, beginning to sweat. This is one of the reasons why I'm no hero — because even though I walked down that corridor toward the creature, I pulled Bastille along with me. I figured two targets were better than one.

As we moved forward, Kaz trailing behind, Bastille lost a bit of her frenzied look. She pulled her dagger from its sheath, the crystalline blade sparkling in the flickering lamplight.

At the end of the corridor was a small room, split in half by the large iron grate. The Scrivener's Bone was on the other side of the bars. He smiled as I approached— one side of his face curling up, lips leering. The other side of his face mimicked the motion, though it was made of bits of metal that twisted and clicked, like a clock mechanism that had been compressed tenfold until all of the gears and pins were smushed together.

"Smedry," the thing said, voice ragged, as if the sounds themselves had been flayed.

"Who are you?" I asked.

The creature met my eyes. The entire left half of its body had been replaced by the bits of metal, held together by a force I didn't understand. One of its eyes was human. The other was a pit of dark glass. Alivener's Glass.

"I am Kilimanjaro," the creature said. "I have been sent to retrieve something from you."

I was still wearing the Lenses of Rashid. I raised my fingers to them, and Kiliman nodded.

"Where did you get that sword?" I asked, trying to hide my nervousness.

"I have the woman," the creature said. "I took it from her."

"She's here, Alcatraz," Bastille said. "I can feel her Fleshstone."

Fleshstone? I thought. *What in the name of the first sands is that?*

"You mean this?" Kiliman asked, voice deep and crackling. He held up something before him. It looked like a crystal shard, about the size of two fingers put together. It was bloody.

Bastille gasped. "No!" she said, rushing toward the bars; I grabbed her arm and barely managed to hang on.

"Bastille!" I said. "He's goading you!"

"How could you?" she screamed at the creature. "You'll kill her!"

Kiliman lowered the crystal, placing it in a pouch at his belt. He still held the sword in front of him. "Death is immaterial, Crystin. I must retrieve what I seek. You have it, and I have the woman. We will trade."

Bastille fell to her knees, and at first I thought she was weeping. Then I could see that she was simply shaking, white faced. I didn't know it at the time, but pulling the Fleshstone from the body of a Crystin is an unspeakably vulgar and gruesome act. To Bastille, it was like Kiliman had shown her Draulin's heart, still beating in his hand.

"You think I'd bargain with *you*?" I asked.

"Yes," Kiliman said simply. He didn't have the flair of evil that Blackburn had shown — no flaunted arrogance, no sharp clothing, or laughing voice. Yet, the quiet danger this creature expressed was somehow even more haunting. I shivered.

"Careful, Al," Kaz said quietly. "Those creatures are dangerous. *Very* dangerous."

Kiliman smiled, then dropped the sword and flipped a hand forward. I cried out as I saw a Lens in his hand. It flashed, shooting out a beam of frosty light.

Bastille came up, her dagger held clawlike in her hand. She took the beam straight on the crystalline blade, then stumbled backward. She held it, but just barely.

I growled, throwing off the Translator's Lenses and pulling out my Windstormer's Lenses. He wanted to fight? Well, I'd show him.

I snapped the Lenses on, then focused on the Scrivener's Bone, sending forth a wave of powerful wind. My ears popped, and Kaz cried out from the sudden increase in pressure. The blast of wind hit Kiliman, throwing him backward, spraying bits of metal from his body.

Kiliman growled, and his Frostbringer's Lens turned off. To my side, Bastille fell to her knees again; I could see that her hand looked blue and was crusted with ice. Her little dagger's blade was cracked in several places. Like the Crystin swords, it could deflect Oculatory powers, but it obviously wasn't meant to handle much punishment.

Kiliman righted himself, and I could see the bits of metal that had fallen off of him spring up little spiderlike legs. The nuts, screws, and gears scuttled across the floor, climbing up his body and rejoining with the entire pulsing, undulating heap of metal scraps.

He met my eyes and growled, bringing up his other hand. I focused again, blasting him with another wave of wind, but the creature stayed on his feet. Suddenly, I felt myself being pulled forward. His other hand held the Lens that Bastille had called a Voidstormer's Lens, the one that sucked in air.

The Lens was pulling me toward the bars, even though I was pushing Kiliman away with my own Lenses. I slipped on the ground, stumbling, growing panicked.

Suddenly, hands grabbed me from behind, steadying me. "What did I tell you, kid?" Kaz called over the sound of the wind. "That thing is part Alivened! You can't kill him with regular means! And those are blood-forged Lenses he's using. They'll be more powerful than yours!"

He was right. Even with Kaz holding on to me, I could feel myself being pulled toward Kiliman. I turned my

Windstormer's Lenses away from him, then focused them on the wall, pushing myself back.

Kiliman turned his Lens off.

I was shaken by the force of the wind blowing from my face. I stumbled, knocking Kaz over, and I nearly lost my footing as I turned my Lenses off.

In that moment, Kiliman focused *his* Lens directly at the pair of Translator's Lenses in my other hand. Apparently, the Voidstormer's Lens — just like my Windstormer's Lenses — could focus on a single object. The Translator's Lenses were pried free from my fingers and sucked across the room.

I yelled, shocked, but Bastille snatched the Lenses from the air as they passed her. She stood up, dagger in one hand, Lenses in the other. I stepped up beside her, readying my Windstormer's Lenses, trying not to look at the frosty wounds on Bastille's hand.

Kiliman stood up, but did not raise his Lenses. "I still hold the knight," he whispered, picking up the fallen Crystin sword. "She will die, for you don't know where to find her. Only I can replace her Fleshstone."

The room fell silent. Suddenly, Kiliman's face began to disintegrate, the tiny bits of metal all springing legs and crawling down his body. Half of his head, then his shoulder, and finally one arm all transformed to tiny, metal spiders, which crawled across the bars separating us, swarming like bees in a hive.

"She will die," the Scrivener's Bone said, somehow speaking despite the fact that half of his face was now missing. "I do not lie, Smedry. You know I do not lie."

I stared him down, but felt an increasing sense of dread. Do you remember what I said about choices? It seems to me that no matter what you choose, you end up losing something. In this case, it was either the Lenses or Draulin's life.

"I will trade her to you for the Lenses," Kiliman said. "I was sent to hunt those, not you. Once I have them, I will leave."

The metal spiders were crawling into the room, crossing the floor, but they stayed away from Bastille and me. Kaz groaned, finally getting to his feet from where I'd inadvertently pushed him.

I closed my eyes. Bastille's mother, or the Lenses? I wished that I could do something to fight. But, the Windstormer's Lenses couldn't hurt this thing — even if they blew him back, he could simply flee and wait for

238

Draulin to die. Australia was still lost somewhere in the Library. Would she be next?

"I will trade," I said quietly.

Kiliman smiled — or, at least, the remaining half of his face smiled. Then, to the side, I saw several of his spiders climb up on something.

A trip wire in the room where I was standing.

The floor fell away beneath Bastille and me as the spiders tripped the wire. Bastille cried out, reaching for the edge of the floor, but she just barely missed grabbing it.

"Rocky Mountain Oysters!" Kaz swore in shock, though the pit opened a few feet away from him. I caught one last glimpse of his panicked face as I tumbled into the hole.

We plummeted some thirty feet and landed with a thud on a patch of too-soft ground. I hit on my stomach, but Bastille — who twisted herself to protect the Translator's Lenses she still clutched — scraped against the wall, then hit the ground in a much more awkward position. She grunted in pain.

I shook my head, trying to clear it. Then, I crawled over to Bastille. She groaned, looking even more dazed than I felt, but she seemed all right. Finally, I glanced up the dark shaft toward the light above. A concerned Kaz stuck his head out over the opening.

"Alcatraz!" he yelled. "You two all right?"

"Yeah," I called up. "I think we are." I poked at the ground, trying to decide why it had broken our fall. It appeared to be made of some kind of cushioned cloth.

"The ground is padded," I called up to Kaz. "Probably to keep us from breaking our necks." It was another Curator trap, meant to frustrate us, but not kill us.

"What was the point of that?" I heard Kaz bellow at Kiliman. "They just agreed to trade with you!"

"Yes, he did." I could faintly hear Kiliman's voice. "But the Librarians of my order have a saying: Never trust a Smedry."

"Well, he's not going to be able to trade with you while he's trapped in a pit!" Kaz yelled.

"True," Kiliman said. "But *you* can trade. Have him pass you the Translator's Lenses, then meet me at the center of the Library. You are the one who has the power to Travel places, are you not?"

Kaz fell silent.

This creature knows a lot about us, I thought with frustration.

"You are a Smedry," Kiliman said to Kaz. "But not an Oculator. I will deal with you instead of the boy. Bring me the Lenses, and I will return the woman — with her Fleshstone — to you. Be quick. She will die within the hour."

There was silence, broken only by Bastille's groan as she sat up. She still had the Translator's Lenses in her hand. Eventually, Kaz's head popped out above the pit.

"Alcatraz?" he called. "You there?"

"Yeah," I said.

"Where else would we be?" Bastille grumbled.

"It's too dark to see you," Kaz said. "Anyway, the Scrivener's Bone has left, and I can't get through the bars to follow him. What should we do? Do you want me to try to find some rope?"

I sat, trying — with all of my capacity — to think of a way out of the predicament. Bastille's mother was dying because a piece of crystal had been ripped from her body. Kiliman had her and would trade her only for the Translator's Lenses. I was trapped in a pit with Bastille, who had taken a much harder hit falling than I had, and we had no rope.

I was stuck, looking for a solution where there wasn't

one. Sometimes, there just isn't a way out, and thinking won't help, no matter how clever you are. In a way, that's kind of like what I wrote at the beginning of this chapter. You remember, the secret "thing" I claimed to have done in this book? The shameful, clever trick? Did you go looking for it? Well, whatever you found, that wasn't what I was intending — because there is no trick. No hidden message. No clever twist I put into the first fourteen chapters.

I don't know how hard you searched, but it couldn't have been harder than I searched for a way to both save Draulin and keep my Lenses. I was quickly running out of time, and I knew it. I had to make a decision. Right then. Right there.

I chose to take the Lenses from Bastille and throw them up to Kaz. He caught them, just barely.

"Can your Talent take you to the center of the Library?" I asked.

He nodded. "I think so. Now that I have a location to search for."

"Go," I said. "Trade the Lenses for Draulin's life. We'll worry about getting them back later."

Kaz nodded. "All right. You wait here — I'll find a rope or

something and come back for you once Bastille's mother is safe."

He disappeared for a moment, then returned, head sticking back out over the opening. "Before I go, do you want this?" He held out Bastille's pack.

The Grappler's Glass boots were inside. I felt a stab of hope, but quickly dismissed it. The sides of the shaft were stone.

Besides, even if I did get free, I'd still have to trade the Lenses for Draulin. I'd just have to do it in person. Still, there was food in the pack. No telling how long we'd be in the pit. "Sure," I called up to him, "drop it."

He did so, and I stepped to the side, letting it hit the soft ground. By now, Bastille was on her feet, though she leaned woozily against the side of the pit.

This was why I shouldn't ever have been made a leader. This is why nobody should ever look to me. Even then, I made the wrong decisions. A leader has to be hard, capable of making the right choice.

You think I *did* make the right one? Well, then, you'd be as poor a leader as I was. You see, saving Draulin was the *wrong* choice. By trading the Translator's Lenses, I may have saved one life, but at a terrible cost.

The Librarians would gain access to the knowledge of the Incarna people. Sure, Draulin would live — but how many would die as the war turned against the Free Kingdoms? With ancient technology at their disposal, the Librarians would become a force that could no longer be held back.

I'd saved one life, but doomed so many more. That's not the sort of weakness a leader can afford. I suspect that Kaz knew the truth of that. He hesitated, then asked, "You sure you want to do this, kid?"

"Yes," I said. At the time, I didn't think about things like protecting the future of the Free Kingdoms or the like. I just knew one thing: I couldn't be the one responsible for Draulin's death.

"All right," Kaz said. "I'll be back for you. Don't worry."

"Good luck, Kaz."

And he was gone.

CHAPTER 16

Writers — particularly storytellers like myself — write about people. That is ironic, since we actually know nothing about them.

Think about it. Why does someone become a writer? Is it because they *like* people? Of course not. Why else would we seek out a job where we get to spend all day, every day, cooped up in our basement with no company besides paper, a pencil, and our imaginary friends?

Writers hate people. If you've ever met a writer, you know that they're generally awkward, slovenly individuals who live beneath stairwells, hiss at those who pass, and forget to bathe for weeklong periods. And those are the socially competent ones.

I looked up at the sides of our pit.

Bastille sat on the floor, obviously trying to pretend she was a patient person. It worked about as well as a watermelon trying to pretend it was a golf ball. (Though not as messy and half as much fun.)

"Come on, Bastille," I said, glancing at her. "I know you're as frustrated as I am. What are you thinking? Could I break these walls somehow? Make a slope we can climb up?"

"And risk the sides of the wall toppling down on us?" she asked flatly.

She had a point. "What if we tried to climb up without using the Talent?"

"These walls are slick and polished, Smedry," she snapped. "Not even a Crystin can climb that."

"But if we shimmied up, feet on one wall, back against the other one . . ."

"The hole is *way* too wide for that."

I fell silent.

"What?" she asked. "No other brilliant ideas? What about *jumping* up? You should try that a few times." She turned away from me, looking at the side of our pit, then sighed.

I frowned. "Bastille, this isn't like you."

"Oh?" she asked. "How do you know what's 'like me' and what isn't? You've known me for what, a couple of months? During which time we've spent all of three or four days together?"

"Yes, but . . . well, I mean . . ."

"It's over, Smedry," she said. "We're beaten. Kaz has probably already arrived at the center of the Library and given up those Lenses. Chances are, Kiliman will just take him captive and let my mother die."

"Maybe we can still find a way out. And go help."

Bastille didn't seem to be listening. She simply sat down, arms folded across her knees, staring at the wall. "They really are right about me," she whispered. "I never deserved to be a knight."

"What?" I asked, squatting down beside her. "Bastille, that's nonsense."

"I've only done two real operations. This one and the infiltration back in your hometown. Both times I ended up trapped, unable to do anything. I'm useless."

"We *all* got trapped," I said. "Your mother didn't fare much better."

She ignored this, still shaking her head. "Useless. You had to save me from those ropes, and then you had to save me *again* when we were covered in tar. That's not even counting the time you saved me from falling out the side of the *Dragonaut.*"

"You saved me too," I said. "Remember the coins? If it wasn't for you, I'd be floating around with burning eyes, offering illicit books to people as if I were a drug dealer looking for a new victim."

(Hey, kids? Want a taste of Dickens? It's awesome, man. Come on. First chapters of *Hard Times* are free. I know you'll be back for *Tale of Two Cities* later.)

"That was different," Bastille said.

"No, it wasn't. Look, you saved my life — not only that, but without you, I wouldn't know what half these Lenses are supposed to do."

She looked up at me, brow furled. "You're doing it again."

"What?"

"Encouraging people. Like you did with Australia, like you've done with all of us this entire trip. What is it about you, Smedry? You don't want to make any decisions, but you take it upon yourself to encourage us all anyway?"

I fell silent. How had that happened? This conversation had been about her, and suddenly she'd thrown it back in my face. (I've found that throwing things in people's

248

faces — words, conversations, knives — is one of Bastille's specialties.)

I looked toward the light flickering faintly in the room above. It seemed haunting and inviting, and as I watched it, I realized something about myself. While I hated being trapped because I worried about what might happen to Kaz and Draulin, there was a larger cause of my frustration.

I wanted to be helping. I didn't want to be left out. I wanted to be in charge. Leaving things to others was tough for me.

"I *do* want to be a leader, Bastille," I whispered.

She rustled, turning to look at me.

"I think all people, in their hearts, want to be heroes," I continued. "But, the ones who want it most are the outcasts. The boys who sit in the backs of rooms, always laughed at because they're different, because they stand out, because . . . they break things."

I wondered if Kaz understood that there were more ways than one to be abnormal. Everyone was strange in some way — everyone had weaknesses that could be mocked. I *did* know how he felt. I'd felt it too.

I didn't want to go back.

"Yes, I want to be a hero," I said. "Yes, I want to be the leader. I used to sit and dream of being the one that people looked to. Of being the one who could *fix* things, rather than break them."

"Well, you have it," she said. "You're the heir to the Smedry line. You're in charge."

"I know. And that terrifies me."

She regarded me. She'd taken off her Warrior's Lenses, and I could see the light from above reflecting in her solemn eyes.

I sat down, shaking my head. "I don't know what to do, Bastille. Being the kid who's always in trouble didn't exactly prepare me for this. How do I decide whether or not to trade my most powerful weapon to save someone's life? I feel like . . . like I'm drowning. Like I'm swimming in water over my head and can't ever reach the top.

"I guess that's why I keep saying I don't want to lead. Because I know if people pay *too* much attention to me, they'll realize that I'm doing a terrible job." I grimaced. "Just like I am now. You and I captured, your mother dying, Kaz walking into danger, and Australia — who *knows* where she is."

I fell silent, feeling even more foolish now that I'd explained it. Yet, oddly, Bastille didn't laugh at me.

"I don't think you're doing a terrible job, Alcatraz," she said. "Being in charge *is* hard. If everything goes well, then nobody pays attention. Yet, if something goes wrong, you're always to blame. I think you've done fine. You just need to be a little bit more sure of yourself."

I shrugged. "Maybe. What do you know of it, anyway?"

"I . . ."

I glanced at her, the tone in her voice making me curious. Some things about Bastille had never added up, in my estimation. She seemed to *know* too much. True, she'd said that she'd wanted to be an Oculator, but that didn't give me enough of an explanation. There was more.

"You *do* know about it," I said.

Now it was her turn to shrug. "A little bit."

I cocked my head.

"Haven't you noticed?" she asked, looking at me. "My mother doesn't have a prison name."

"So?"

"So, I do."

I scratched my head.

"You really *don't* know anything, do you?" she asked.

I snorted. "Well, excuse me for being raised on a completely different continent from you people. What are you talking about?"

"You are named Alcatraz after Alcatraz the First," Bastille said. "The Smedries use names like that a lot, names from their heritage. The Librarians, then, have tried to discredit those names by using them for prisons."

"You're not a Smedry," I said, "but you have a prison name too."

"Yes, but my family is also . . . traditional. They tend to use famous names over and over again, just like your family does. That's not something that common people do."

I blinked.

Bastille rolled her eyes. "My father's a nobleman, Smedry," she said. "That's what I'm trying to tell you. I have a traditional name because I'm his daughter. My full name is Bastille Vianitelle the Ninth."

"Ah, right." It's sort of like what rich people, kings, and popes do in the Hushlands — they reuse old names, then just add a number.

"I grew up with everyone expecting me to be a leader," she said. "Only, I'm not very well suited to it. Not like you."

"I'm not well suited to it!"

She snorted. "You are good with people, Smedry. Me, I don't *want* to lead people. They kind of annoy me."

"You should have become a novelist."

"Don't like the hours," she said. "Anyway, I can tell you that growing up learning how to lead doesn't make any difference. A lifetime of training only makes you understand just how inadequate you are."

We fell silent.

"So . . . what happened?" I asked. "How did you end up as a Crystin?"

"My mother," Bastille said. "She's not noble, but she *is* a Crystin. She always pushed me to become a Knight of Crystallia, saying that my father didn't need another useless daughter hanging about. I tried to prove her wrong, but I'm too well-bred to do something simple, like become a baker or a carpenter."

"So you tried to become an Oculator."

She nodded. "I didn't tell anyone. I'd heard that Oculatory power was genetic, of course, but I intended to prove everyone wrong. I'd be the first Oculator in my line, then my mother and father would be impressed.

"Well, you know how that turned out. So, I just joined

the Crystin, like my mother had always said I should. I had to give up my title and my money. Now I'm realizing just how foolish that decision was. I make an even worse Crystin than I did an Oculator."

She sighed, folding her arms again. "The thing is, I thought — for a while — that I *would* be good at it. I made knight faster than anyone ever had. Then, I was immediately sent out to protect the Old Smedry — which was one of the most dangerous, difficult assignments the knights had. I *still* don't know why they picked that as my first job. It's never made sense."

"It's almost like they were setting you up to fail."

She sat for a moment. "I never thought about it that way. Why would anyone do such a thing?"

I shrugged. "I don't know. But, you have to admit, it does sound suspicious. Maybe someone in charge of giving the assignments was jealous of how quickly you made it to knight, and wanted to see you fall."

"At the cost, maybe, of the Old Smedry's life?"

I shrugged. "People do strange things sometimes, Bastille."

"I still find it hard to believe," she said. "Besides, my mother was part of the group that makes those assignments."

"She seems like a hard one to please."

Bastille snorted. "That's an understatement. I made knight, and all she could say was, 'Make certain you live up to the honor.' I think she was *expecting* me to bungle my first job — maybe that's why she came to get me herself."

I didn't reply, but somehow I knew we were thinking the same thing. Bastille's own *mother* couldn't have been the one to set her up to fail, could she? That seemed a stretch. Of course, my mother had stolen my inheritance, then sold me out to the Librarians. So, maybe Bastille and I were a well-matched pair.

I sat with my back against the wall, looking up, and my mind turned away from Bastille's problems and back to what I'd said earlier. It had felt good to get the thoughts out. It had helped me, finally, sort out how I felt. A few months back, I would have settled for simply being normal. Now I knew that being a Smedry meant something. The more time I spent filling that role, the more I wanted to do it well. To justify the name I bore, and live up to what my grandfather and the others expected of me.

Perhaps you find that ironic. There I was, deciding bravely that I would take upon myself the mantle that had been quite randomly thrust upon me. Now, here I am, writing my memoirs, trying as hard as I can to throw off that very same mantle.

I *wanted* to be famous. That should, in itself, be enough to make you worried. Never trust a man who wants to be a hero. We'll talk about this more in the next book.

"We're quite the pair, aren't we?" Bastille asked, smiling for the first time I'd seen since we fell down the shaft.

I smiled back. "Yeah. Why is it that my best soul-searching moments always come when I'm trapped?"

"Sounds like you should be imprisoned more often."

I nodded. Then, I jumped as something floated out of the wall next to me. "Gak!" I said before I realized it was just a Curator.

"Here," it said, dropping a leaf of paper to the ground.

"What's this?" I asked, picking it up.

"Your book."

It was the paper I'd written in the tomb, the inscription about the Dark Talent. That meant we'd been trapped for nearly an hour. Bastille was right. Kaz had probably already reached the center of the Library.

The Curator floated away.

"Your mother," I said, folding up the paper. "If she gets that crystal thing back, she'll be all right?"

Bastille nodded.

"So, since we're trapped here with no hope of rescue, do you mind telling me what that crystal was? You know, to help pass the time?"

Bastille snorted, then stood up and pulled the silvery hair up off the back of her neck. She turned around, and I could see a sparkling blue crystal set into the skin on the back of her neck. I could see it easily, as she still only wore the tight black T-shirt tucked into the trousers of her militaristic uniform.

"Wow," I said.

"Three kinds of crystals grow in Crystallia," she said, letting her hair back down. "The first we turn into swords and daggers. The second become Fleshstones, which are what really make us into Crystin."

"What does it do?" I asked.

Bastille paused. "Things," she finally replied.

"How wonderfully specific."

She flushed. "It's kind of personal, Alcatraz. It's because of the Fleshstone that I can run so quickly. Stuff like that."

"Okay," I said. "And the third type of crystal?"

"Also personal."

Great, I thought.

"It's not really important," she said. As she moved to sit down, I noticed something. Her hand — the one that had been holding the dagger that had blocked the Frostbringer's Lens — had red and cracking skin.

"You okay?" I asked, nodding to her hand.

"I'll be fine," she said. "Our daggers are made from immature swordstones — they aren't meant to hold out against powerful Lenses for long. A little of the ice got around and hit my fingers, but it's nothing that won't heal."

I wasn't as convinced. "Maybe you should —"

"Hush!" Bastille said suddenly, climbing to her feet.

I did so, frowning. I followed Bastille's gaze up toward the top of our hole.

"What?" I asked.

"I thought I heard something," she replied.

We waited tensely. Finally, we saw shadows moving above. Bastille slowly pulled her dagger from its sheath, and even in the darkness, I could see that it was laced with cracks. What she expected to do at such a distance was beyond me.

Finally, a head leaned out over the hole.

"Hello?" Australia asked. "Anybody down there?"

CHAPTER 17

I hope you didn't find the last line of that previous chapter to be exciting. It was simply a convenient place to end.

You see, chapter breaks are, in a way, like Smedry Talents. They defy time and space. (This, alone, should be enough to prove to you that traditional Hushlander physics is just a load of unwashed underpants.)

Think about it. By putting in a chapter break, I make the book longer. It takes extra spaces, extra pages. Yet, because of those chapter breaks, the book becomes *shorter* as well. You read it more quickly. Even an unexciting hook, like Australia's showing up, encourages you to quickly turn the page and keep going.

Space becomes distorted when you read a book. Time has less relevance. In fact, if you look closely, you might be able to see golden dust floating down around you right now. (And if you can't see it, you're just not trying hard enough. Maybe you need to hit yourself on the head with another big thick fantasy novel.)

"We're down here!" I yelled up to Australia. Beside me, Bastille looked relieved and slipped her dagger back into its sheath.

"Alcatraz?" Australia asked. "Uh . . . what are you doing down there?"

"Having a tea party," I yelled back. "What do you think? We're trapped!"

"Silly," she said. "Why'd you go and get trapped?"

I glanced at Bastille. She just rolled her eyes. That's Australia for you.

"We didn't exactly have a choice," I called back.

"I climbed a tree once and couldn't get back down," Australia said. "I guess it's kind of the same, right?"

"Sure," I said. "Look, I need you to find some rope."

"Uh," she said. "Where exactly am I going to find something like that?"

"I don't know!"

"All right, then." She sighed loudly and disappeared.

"She's hopeless," Bastille said.

"I'm realizing that. At least she's still got her soul. I was half afraid that she'd end up in serious trouble."

"Like getting captured by a member of the Scrivener's Bones, or perhaps falling down a pit?"

"Something like that," I said, kneeling down. I wasn't about to count on Australia to get us out. I'd already been around her long enough to realize that she probably wasn't going to be of much help.

(Which, incidentally, was why you shouldn't have been all that excited to see her show up. You still turned the page, didn't you?)

I opened Bastille's pack and pulled out the boots with the Grappler's Glass on the bottom. I activated the glass, then stuck a boot to the side of the wall. As expected, it didn't stick. They only worked on glass.

"So . . . maybe we *should* have you try to break the walls down," Bastille said speculatively. "You'll probably bury us in stone, but that would be better than sitting around talking about our feelings and that nonsense."

I glanced over, smiling.

"What?" she asked.

"Nothing," I said. "Just good to have you back."

She snorted. "Well? Breaking? Can you do it?"

"I can try," I said speculatively. "But, well, it seems like a long shot."

"We've never had to depend on one of *those* before," she said.

"Good point." I rested my hands against the wall.

The Dark Talent . . . beware it. . . .

The words from the tomb wall returned to my mind. The paper with the inscription sat in my pocket, but I tried not to think about it. Now that I'd begun to understand what my Talent was, it didn't seem a good time to start second-guessing its nature.

There would be time enough for that later.

I tentatively sent a wave of breaking power into the wall. Cracks twisted away from my palms, moving through the stone. Bits of dust and chips began to fall in on us, but I kept going. The wall groaned.

"Alcatraz!" Bastille said, grabbing my arm and pulling me back.

I stumbled back, dazed, away from the wall as a large chunk of stone toppled inward and hit the floor where I had been standing. The soft, springy ground gave way beneath the stone. Kind of like my head would have, had it been in the way. Only that would have involved a lot more blood and a lot more screaming.

I stared at the chunk of stone. Then, I glanced up at the wall. It was cracked and broken, and other bits of it seemed ready to fall off too.

"Okay, that was expected," Bastille said, "but still kind of dumb of us, eh?"

I nodded, stooping over to pick up a Grappler's boot. If only I could get it to work. I put it up against the wall again, but it refused to stick.

"That's not going to do anything, Smedry," Bastille said.

"There's silicon in the rock. That's the same thing as glass."

"True," Bastille said. "But there isn't enough to make the Grappler's Glass stick."

I tried anyway. I focused on the glass, closing my eyes, treating it like it was a pair of Lenses.

During the months Grandpa Smedry had been training me, I'd learned how to activate stubborn Lenses. There was a trick to it. You had to give them energy. Pour part of yourself into them to make them function.

Come on! I thought to the boot, pressing it to the wall. *There's glass in the wall. Little bits of it. You can stick. You* have to *stick.*

I'd contacted Grandpa Smedry at a much greater distance than I was supposed to be able to. I'd done that by focusing hard on my Courier's Lenses, somehow giving them an extra boost of power. Could I somehow do the same to this boot?

I thought I felt something. The boot, pulling slightly toward the wall. I focused harder, straining, feeling myself grow tired. Yet, I didn't give up. I continued to push, opening my eyes and staring intently.

The glass on the bottom of the boot began to glow softly. Bastille looked over, shocked.

Come on, I thought again. I felt the boot drawing something from me, taking it out, feeding on it.

When I carefully pulled my hand away, the boot stayed where it was.

"Impossible," Bastille whispered, walking over.

I wiped my brow, smiling triumphantly.

Bastille reached out with a careful touch, poking the boot. Then, she easily pulled it off the wall.

"Hey!" I said. "Did you see what I had to go through to get that to stick?"

She snorted. "It came off easily, Smedry. Do you honestly expect that you'd be able to walk up the wall with it?"

I felt my sense of triumph deflate. She was right. If I had to work *that* hard to get one boot to stay in one place, there was no way I'd be able to summon enough effort to get all the way to the top.

"Still," Bastille said. "That's pretty amazing. How did you do it?"

I shrugged. "I just shoved a little extra power into the glass."

Bastille didn't reply. She stared at the boot, then looked at me. "This is silimatic," she said. "Technology, not magic. You shouldn't be able to push it like that. Technology has limits."

"I think your technology and your magic are more related than people believe, Bastille," I said.

She nodded slowly. Then, she moved quickly, putting the boot back into the pack and zipping it up. "You still have those Windstormer's Lenses?" she asked.

"Yeah," I said. "Why?"

She looked up, meeting my eyes. "I have an idea."

"Should I be frightened?" I asked.

"Probably," she said. "The idea's a little bit strange. Like one you might have come up with, actually."

I raised an eyebrow.

"Get out those Lenses," she said, throwing her pack over her shoulder.

I did so.

"Now, break the frames."

I paused, eyeing her.

"Just do it," she said.

I shrugged, then activated my Talent. The frames fell apart easily.

"Double up the Lenses," she said.

"Okay," I said, sliding one over the other.

"Can you do to those Lenses what you did to the boots? Put extra power through them?"

"I should be able to," I said. "But . . ."

I trailed off, suddenly coming to understand. If I blew a huge blast of air out of the Lenses, then I would be forced upward — like a fighter jet, with the Lenses being my engine. I looked up at Bastille. "Bastille! That's absolutely insane."

"I know," she said, grimacing. "I've been spending *way* too much time with you Smedries. But my mother is probably only a few minutes away from death. Are you willing to give it a try?"

I smiled. "Of course I am! It sounds awesome!"

Inclined toward leadership or not, thoughtful or not, uncertain of myself or not, I was still a teenage boy. And, you have to admit, it really did sound awesome.

Bastille stepped up close to me, putting one arm around my waist, then holding on to my shoulder with the other. "Then I'm going with you," she said. "Hang on to my waist."

I nodded, feeling a bit distracted having her so close. For the first time in my life, I realized something.

Girls smell weird.

I started to feel nervous. If I blew with the Lenses too softly, we'd just fall back down into the pit. If I blasted too hard, we'd end up smashing into the ceiling. It seemed like a very fine balance.

I lowered my arm, pointing the Lenses down straight by my side, my other arm held tentatively around Bastille's waist. I took a breath, preparing myself.

"Smedry," Bastille said, her face just inches from mine.

I blinked. Having her right there was suddenly really, *really* distracting. Plus, she was hanging on rather tightly, with the grip of a person whose strength has been enhanced by a Crystin Fleshstone.

I fumbled for a response, my mind fuzzy. (Girls, you might have noticed, can do things like this to guys. It's a result of their powerful pheromones. They evolved that way, gaining the ability to make us men fuzzy-headed, so that it would be easier for them to hit us on the heads with hardback fantasy novels and steal our cheese sticks.)

"You okay?" she asked.

"Uh . . . yeah," I managed to get out. "What did you want?"

"I just wanted to say thanks."

"For what?"

"For provoking me," she said. "For making me think that someone had set me up to fail on purpose. It's probably not true, but it's what I needed. If there's a chance that someone stuck me in that situation intentionally, then I want to figure out who it was and why they did it. It's a challenge."

I nodded. That's Bastille for you. Tell her that she's wonderful, and she'd just sit there and sulk. But, hint that she might have a hidden enemy somewhere, and she'd jump to her feet, full of energy.

"You ready?" I asked.

"Ready as I'll ever be."

I focused on the Lenses — trying to ignore how close Bastille was — and built up Oculatory energy.

Then, holding my breath, I released the power.

We shot upward in a lurching burst of wind. Dust and chips of stone blew out beneath us, puffing up the sides of the shaft. We blasted upward, wind tussling my hair, the opening to the pit approaching far too quickly. I cried out, deactivating the Lenses, but we had too much momentum.

We passed the lip of the hole and continued on. I threw up my hands in front of my face as we approached the ceiling. With the Lenses no longer jetting, gravity slowed us. We crested the blast a few inches from the ceiling, then began to plummet downward again.

"Now, kick!" Bastille said, twisting and putting both of her feet against my chest.

"Wha —" I began, but Bastille kicked, throwing me to the side and pushing herself the other direction.

We hit the ground on either side of the pit. I rolled, then came to a rest, staring upward. The room spun around me.

We were free. I sat up, holding my head. Across the pit, Bastille was smiling as she jumped to her feet. "I can't believe that actually worked!"

"You kicked me!" I said with a groan.

"Well, I owed it to you," she said. "Remember, you kicked me back in the *Dragonaut.* I didn't want you to feel like I didn't return the feeling."

I grimaced. This, by the way, is a pretty good metaphor for my entire relationship with Bastille. I'm thinking of writing a book on the concept. *Kicking Your Friends for Fun and Profit.*

Suddenly, something occurred to me. "My Lenses!" They lay in shattered pieces on the ground beside the pit. I'd dropped them as I hit. I stood up and rushed over, but it was no use. There wasn't enough of them left to use.

"Gather up the pieces," Bastille said. "They can be reforged."

I sighed. "Yeah, I suppose. This means we're going to have to face Kiliman without them."

Bastille fell silent.

I don't have any offensive Lenses, and Bastille's only got a close-to-broken dagger. How are we going to fight that creature?

I brushed the pieces of glass into a pouch, then put it into one of my Lens pockets.

"We're free," Bastille said, "but we still don't really know what to do. In fact, we don't even know how to get to Kiliman."

"We'll find a way," I said, standing up.

She looked at me, then — surprisingly — nodded. "All right, then, what do we do?"

"We —"

Suddenly, Australia rushed back into the room. She was puffing from exertion. "All right, I found your rope!"

She held up an empty hand.

"Uh, thanks," I said. "Is the rope imaginary, then?"

"No, silly," she said, laughing. She picked something up between two fingers. "Look!"

"Trip wire," Bastille said.

"Is that what it is?" Australia said. "I just found it on the ground over there."

"And how exactly were you going to use that to get us out of the pit?" I asked. "I doubt it's long enough, and even if it is, it would never have held our weight."

Australia cocked her head. "*That's* why you wanted rope?"

"Sure," I said. "So that we could climb out of the pit."

"But, you're already out of the pit."

"We are *now,*" I said with exasperation. "But we weren't at the time. I wanted you to find rope so that we could climb it."

"Oh!" Australia said. "Well, you should have said so, then!"

I stood, stupefied. "You know what, never mind," I said, taking the length of trip wire. I was about to stuff it in my pocket, then paused, looking at it.

"What?" Bastille asked.

I smiled.

"You have an idea?"

I nodded.

"What is it?"

"Tell you in a minute," I said. "First, we have to figure out how to get to the center of the Library."

We all looked at one another.

"I've been wandering through the hallways all day," Australia said. "With those ghost things offering me books at every turn. I keep explaining that I *hate* reading, but they don't listen. If I hadn't run across your footprints, Alcatraz, I'd still be lost!"

"Footprints!" I said. "Australia, can you see Kaz's footprints?"

"Of course." She tapped the yellow Lenses, my Tracker's Lenses, which she was still wearing.

"Follow them!"

She nodded, then led us from the room. Only a few feet down the hallway, however, she stopped.

"What?" I asked.

"They end here."

His Talent, I realized. *It's jumping him about the Library, leading him to the center. We'll never be able to track him.*

"That's it, then," Bastille said, beginning to sound depressed again. "We'll never get there in time."

"No," I said. "If I'm in charge, then we're not going to give up."

She looked taken aback. Then, she nodded. "All right. What do we do?"

I stood for a moment, thinking. There had to be a way. *Information, lad,* Grandpa Smedry's voice seemed to return to me. *More powerful than any sword or gun . . .*

I looked up sharply. "Australia, can you follow my footprints back the way I originally came, before I entered that room with the pit?"

"Sure," she said.

"Do it, then."

She led us through cagelike chambers and corridors. In a few minutes, we left the dungeon section of the Library and entered the section with the bookshelves. The gold bars I'd discarded on the ground proved that we were back where we'd started. I, of course, piled the bars into Bastille's pack.

No, not because of some great plan to use them. I just figured that if I survived all this, I'd want some gold. (I don't know if you realize this, but you can totally buy stuff with it.)

"Great," Bastille said. "We're back here. I don't mean to question you, O Great Leader, but we were lost when we were *here* too. We still don't know which way to go."

I reached into a pocket, then pulled out the Discerner's Lenses. I put them on, then looked at the bookshelves. I smiled.

"What?" Bastille asked.

"They hold every book ever written, right?"

"That's what the Curators claim."

"So, they would have gathered them chronologically. When a new book comes out, the Curators get a copy, then put it on their shelves."

"So?"

"That means," I said, "that the newer books are going to be at the outer edges of the Library. The older the books get, the closer we'll get to the center. That's the place where they would have put their first books."

Bastille opened her mouth slightly, then her eyes widened as she understood. "Alcatraz, that's brilliant!"

"Must have been that bump to the head," I said, then pointed down the hallway. "That way. The books get older as they move down the row that direction."

Bastille and Australia nodded, and we were off.

CHAPTER 18

We're almost at the end of the second book. Hopefully, you've enjoyed the ride. I'm certain you know more about the world now than you did when you began.

In fact, you've probably learned all you need to. You know about the Librarian conspiracy, and you know that I'm a liar. Everything I wanted to do has been accomplished. I suppose I can just end the book right here.

Thanks for reading.

The end.

Oh, so that's not good enough for you, eh? Demanding today, are we?

All right, fine. I'll finish it for you. But, not because I'm a nice guy. I'll do it because I can't wait to see the look on your face when Bastille dies. (You didn't forget about that part, did you? I'll bet you think I'm lying. However, I promise you that I'm not. She really dies. You'll see.)

Bastille, Australia, and I raced through the Library hallways. We'd passed through the rooms with books and were up to the ones with scrolls. These too were arranged by age. We were close. I could feel it.

That worried me. Bastille's mother was dying, and Kaz was likely in serious danger. We had little hope in fighting Kiliman. We were outmatched and outmaneuvered, and we were charging right into the enemy's hands.

However, I figured that it wasn't a good idea to explain to the others how bad things seemed. I was determined to keep a "stiff upper lip," even if I didn't really understand what that meant. (Though it does sound vaguely uncomfortable.)

"All right," I said. "We have to beat this guy. What are our resources?" That sounded like the kind of thing a leader would say.

"One cracked dagger," Bastille said. "Probably won't survive another hit from those Frostbringer's Lenses."

"We've got that string," Australia added, poking through Bastille's pack as we ran. "And . . . it looks like a couple of muffins. Oh, and one pair of boots."

Great, I thought. "Well, I'm down to three pairs of Lenses. We've got my Oculator's Lenses — which won't be much good, since Grandpa Smedry *still* hasn't bothered to teach me how to use them defensively. We've got the Discerner's Lenses, which will get us to the center. And we've got Australia's Tracker's Lenses."

"Plus that Lens you found in the tomb," Bastille noted.

"Which, unfortunately, we can't seem to use."

Bastille nodded. "Though, we've also got two Smedries — and two Talents."

"That's right," I said. "Australia, do you have to fall asleep for yours to work?"

"Of course I do, silly," she said. "I can't wake up looking ugly if I don't fall asleep!"

I sighed.

"I'm *really* good at falling asleep," she said.

"Well, that's something at least," I grumbled. Then, I cursed myself. "I mean, bravely onward we must go, troops!"

Bastille shot me a grimace.

"Little too much?"

"Just a smidge," she said drily. "I —"

She cut off as I held up a hand. We skidded to a halt in the musty hallway. To the sides, ancient lamps flickered, and a trio of Curators floated around us, ever present, watching for an opportunity to offer us books.

"What?" Bastille asked.

"I can feel the creature," I said. "At least, his Lenses."

"Then he can feel us?"

I shook my head. "Scrivener's Bones aren't Oculators. Those blood-forged Lenses might make him tough, but we hold the edge in information. We . . ."

I trailed off as I noticed something.

"Alcatraz?" Bastille asked, but I wasn't paying attention.

There, on the wall directly above the archway leading onward, was a set of scribbles. Like those made by a child too young to even draw pictures. To my eyes, they seemed to glow with a pure white color.

That aura came from the Discerner's Lenses. The scribbles were fairly fresh — no older than a couple of days. Compared with the ancient stones and scrolls in the hallway, the scribbles seemed a pure white.

"*Alcatraz*," Bastille hissed. "What's going on?"

"That's the Forgotten Language," I said, pointing to the scribbles.

"What?"

To her eyes, the scribbles would be almost invisible — only the Discerner's Lenses had let me see them so starkly.

"Look closer," I said.

Eventually, she nodded. "Okay, so I think I see some lines up there. What of it?"

"They're new," I said. "Written within the last few days. So, if that really *is* the Forgotten Language, then only someone wearing Translator's Lenses could have written it."

Finally, she seemed to understand. "And that means . . ."

"My father was here." I looked back up at the marks. "And I can't read the message he left for me because I gave my Lenses away."

Our group fell silent.

My father has Lenses that let him glimpse the future. Could he have left me a message to help me fight Kiliman?

I felt frustrated. There was no way to read the inscription. If my father *had* seen into the future, wouldn't he have realized I wouldn't have my Lenses?

No — Grandpa Smedry had said that Oracle's Lenses were very unreliable and gave inconsistent information. My father very well *could* have seen that I'd be fighting Kiliman, but not known that I'd be without my Translator's Lenses.

Just to be certain, I tried the Lens I'd found in the tomb of Alcatraz the First. But, it wasn't a Translator's Lens, so it didn't let me read the inscription. Sighing, I put it away.

Information. I didn't have it. Finally, I began to grasp what Grandpa Smedry kept saying. The person who won the battle wasn't necessarily the one with the biggest army or the best weapons — it was the one who understood the most about the situation.

"Alcatraz," Bastille said. "Please. My mother . . ."

I glanced at her. Bastille is strong. Her toughness isn't just an act, like it is with some people. Yet, I've seen her really, truly worried on a number of occasions. It's always when someone she loves is in danger.

I wasn't sure if Draulin deserved that loyalty, but I wasn't going to question a girl's love for her mother.

"Right," I said. "Sorry. We'll come back for this later."

Bastille nodded. "You want me to go scout?"

"Yeah. Be careful. I can feel Kiliman just ahead."

She needed no further warning. I turned toward Australia. "How quickly can you fall asleep?"

"Oh, in about five minutes."

"Get to it, then," I said.

"Who should I think about?" she asked. "That'll be the person I look like when I wake up." She grimaced at that concept.

"It depends," I said. "How flexible *is* your Talent? What kinds of things can you become, if you try?"

"I once dreamed about a hot day and I woke up as a Popsicle."

Well, I thought, *that's one thing she's got on me.* Either way, it meant that the Talent was pretty darn flexible — more so than Kaz had given it credit.

Bastille was back a few seconds later. "He's there," she whispered. "Talking into a Courier's Lens, but not making much progress because of the Library's interference. I think he's seeking direction about what to do with you."

"Your mother?"

"Tied up on the side of the room," Bastille said. "They're in a large, circular chamber with scroll cases running along the outside. Alcatraz . . . he's got Kaz too, tied up with my mother. Kaz can't use his Talent if he can't move."

"Your mother?" I asked. "How's she look?"

Bastille's expression grew dark. "It was hard to tell from the distance, but I could see that she hasn't been healed yet. Kiliman must still have her Fleshstone." She pulled her dagger from its sheath.

I grimaced, then glanced at Australia.

"So, who am I supposed to look like again?" she asked, yawning. To her credit, she already looked drowsy.

"Put away that dagger, Bastille," I said. "We're not going to need it."

"It's the only weapon we have!" she protested.

"Actually, it's not. We've got something far, far better. . . ."

★

Are you sure I can't stop the book here? I mean, this next part isn't really all that important. Really.

All right, fine.

Bastille and I dashed into the room. It was just like she had described — wide and circular, with a domed roof and racks of scrolls around the outside. I didn't need the Discerner's Lenses to tell that these scrolls were *old*. It was a wonder they hadn't fallen apart.

A smattering of ghostly Curators moved through the chamber, several of them whispering tempting words to Kaz and Draulin. The captives lay on the ground — Kaz looking furious, Draulin looking sickly and dazed — directly opposite from the doorway Bastille and I came in through.

Kiliman stood near the captives, Crystin sword on an ancient reading table beside him. He looked up when we entered, seeming completely shocked. Even if he'd anticipated trouble, he obviously hadn't been expecting me to charge into the room head-on.

To be honest, I was a little surprised myself.

Kaz began to struggle even harder, and a Curator floated toward him, looming menacingly. Kiliman smiled, flesh lips rising on one side of his twisted face, metal ones rising on the other side. Gears, bolts, and screws shifted around his single, beady glass eye. The Scrivener's Bone immediately grabbed Draulin's crystal sword in one hand, then he pulled out a Lens with the other.

"Thank you, Smedry," he said, "for saving me the trouble of having to go and fetch you."

We charged. To this day, that is probably one of the very most ridiculous sights in which I've ever participated. Two kids, barely into our teens, carrying no visible weapons, charging directly at a seven-foot-tall half-human Librarian with a massive crystalline sword.

We reached him at the same time — Bastille had paced herself to keep from outrunning me — and I felt my heart begin to flutter with anxiety.

What was I doing?

Kiliman swung. At me, of course. I threw myself into a roll, feeling the sword whoosh over my head. At that moment — while Kiliman was distracted — Bastille whipped a boot out of her pack and threw it directly at Kiliman's head.

It hit, sole first. The Grappler's Glass immediately locked onto the glass of Kiliman's left eye. The front tip of the boot extended over the bridge of his nose, jutting out past the side of his face, almost completely obscuring the view out his flesh eye as well.

The Librarian stood for a moment, seeming completely dumbfounded. That was probably the proper reaction for one who had just gotten hit in the face by a large, magical boot. Then he cursed, reaching up awkwardly, trying to pull the boot off of his face.

I scrambled to my feet. Bastille whipped out the second boot, then threw it — her aim dead on — at the pouch on

Kiliman's belt. The boot stuck to the glass inside, and Bastille yanked hard on the trip wire in her hands — which was, of course, tied to the boot.

The pouch ripped free, and Bastille pulled the whole lot — wire, boot, and pouch — back into her hands, like some strange fisherman without enough money to afford a pole. She grinned at me, then pulled open the pouch, triumphantly revealing the crystal inside, stuck to the boot.

She tossed it all to me. I caught the boot, then turned off its glass. The pouch fell into my hand. Inside it, I found the Fleshstone — which I tossed to Bastille — and something else. A Lens.

I pulled it out eagerly. It wasn't, however, my Translator's Lenses. It was just the Tracker's Lens that Kiliman had been using to follow us.

We'll have to worry about the Translator's Lenses later, I thought. *No time right now.*

Kiliman bellowed, finally getting one hand inside the boot, then pulling it free by making as if he were taking a step with the hand. The Grappler's Glass let go, and Kiliman tossed the boot aside.

I gulped. He wasn't supposed to have figured that out so quickly.

"Nice trick," he said, swinging the sword at me again. I scrambled away, dashing back toward the exit. Kiliman, however, just raised his Frostbringer's Lens, getting ready to fire it square into my back.

"Hey, Kiliman!" a voice suddenly yelled. "I'm free and I'm making a face at you!"

Kiliman spun with shock to find Kaz, standing free from his bonds and smiling broadly. A Curator hovered next to him — but this Curator had grown legs and was starting to look more and more like Australia as her Talent wore off. We'd sent her in first, looking like one of the ghosts, to untie the captives.

Kiliman had another moment of dumbfounded shock, which Bastille took advantage of by tossing her mother's Fleshstone to Kaz. The short man caught it, then grabbed one of Draulin's ropes — she was still tied up — while Australia grabbed the other one. Together, they towed the knight behind them, running away.

Kiliman screamed in rage. It was a terrible, half-metallic sound. He spun his Frostbringer's Lens around. The glass was already glowing, and a beam of bluish light shot out.

But Kaz and the other two were already gone, lost by Kaz's Talent, into the netherspaces of the Library.

"Smedry!" Kiliman said, turning back toward me as I reached the doorway. "I will hunt you. Even if you escape me today, I will follow. You will *never* be free of me!"

I paused. Bastille should have already run for freedom. Yet, she still stood in the center of the room, from where she'd tossed the Fleshstone to Kaz.

She was staring at Kiliman. Slowly, he became aware of her presence, and he turned.

Run, Bastille! I thought.

She did. Directly *at* Kiliman.

"No!" I yelled.

Later, when I had time to think about it, I would realize why Bastille did what she did. She knew that Kiliman wasn't lying. He intended to chase us, and he was an expert hunter. He'd probably find us again before we even got out of the Library.

There was only one way to be rid of him. And that was to face him. Now.

I wasn't aware of this reasoning at the time. I just thought she was being stupid. Yet, I did something even more stupid.

I charged back into the room.

CHAPTER 19

Life is not fair.

If you are the discriminating reader that I think you are (you picked up this book, after all), then you should have figured this out. There are very few aspects about life that are, in any way, fair.

It isn't fair that some people are rich and others are poor. It isn't fair that I'm rambling like this, instead of continuing the climax of the story. It isn't fair that I'm so outrageously handsome, while most people are simply ordinary. It isn't fair that *diphthong* gets to be such an awesome-sounding word, yet has to mean something relatively unawesome.

No, life is not fair. It is, however, funny.

The only thing you can do is laugh at it. Some days, you have to sit in your boring chair sipping warm cocoa. Other days, you get to blast your way out of a pit in the ground, and then run off to fight a half-metal monster who is holding your friend's mother captive. Other days, you need to dress like a green hamster and dance around in circles while people throw pomegranates at you.

Don't ask.

There are two lessons I think one should learn from this book. The second one I'll blather on about in the next chapter, but the first one — and perhaps more interesting one — is this: Please remember to laugh. It's good for you. (Plus, while you're laughing, it's easier for me to hit you with the pomegranate.)

Laugh when good things happen. Laugh when bad things happen. Laugh when life is so plain boring that you can't find anything amusing about it beyond the fact that it's so utterly unamusing.

Laugh when books come to a close, even if the endings aren't happy.

This isn't part of the plan, I thought desperately as I dashed back into the room. *What's the point of having a plan if people don't follow it?*

Kiliman activated the Frostbringer's Lens, blasting it toward Bastille. She dropped her pack and whipped up her dagger, slicing it directly through the icy beam. The dagger shattered, and her hand turned blue. But, she blocked the ray long enough to get inside Kiliman's reach, and she delivered a solid blow to his stomach with her other hand.

Kiliman let out an *oof* of pain and stumbled backward. Angered, he slammed his sword down toward Bastille. Somehow, she got out of the way, and the sword hit the ground with a harsh sound.

She's so quick! I thought. She was already around to Kiliman's side and delivered a powerful kick to his ribs. Although he didn't look like he enjoyed the blow, he didn't react as much as I would have thought a regular person would. He was part Alivened; regular weapons couldn't kill this creature. That was a job for an Oculator.

As I grew close, Kiliman spun, slamming his shoulder into Bastille's chest. The blow threw her backward to the ground, and Kiliman laughed, then raised the Frostbringer's Lens, pointing it directly at her.

"No!" I yelled. The only thing I had, however, was the Grappler's Glass boot. So, I threw it.

The Lens began to glow. For once in my life, however, my aim was true — and the boot hit the Lens square on and locked into place. When the Lens went off, ice formed in a large block around the shoe, weighing it down — but also filling the boot itself, making it impossible to reach inside and turn it off.

Kiliman cursed, shaking his hand. As he did so, I realized that I still had ahold of the trip wire tied to the boot. Thinking that I'd be able to pull the Frostbringer's Lens to myself, I yanked on the wire.

I hadn't stopped to think that Kiliman might yank back. And he was a *lot* stronger than I was. His pull caused the wire to bite into my hands as it yanked me off my feet. I cried out, hitting the ground, and my Talent proactively broke the wire before Kiliman could pull me any farther toward him. I looked up, dazed, ten feet of wire still wrapped around my hands.

Kiliman freed his hand from the frozen Lens-boot combination, and he tossed both aside. Bastille was climbing to her feet. Without her jacket — which had broken when the *Dragonaut* crashed — she couldn't take much more punishment than a regular person, and Kiliman had hit her square on with a metal shoulder. It was a wonder she could even walk.

Kiliman hefted the Crystin blade in two hands, then smiled at us. He didn't seem to be at all threatened; that attitude, however, seemed to make Bastille even more determined. Despite my yelled warning, she charged the monster again.

And she calls us Smedries crazy! I thought with frustration, pushing myself to my feet. As Kiliman raised his weapon to swing at Bastille, I slammed my hand to the ground and released the Breaking Talent.

The floor cracked. There was an awesome, deafening sound as rocks shattered and sections of floor became rubble. Kiliman idly stepped to the side, raising a metallic eyebrow at the rift that appeared behind him.

"What, exactly, was that supposed to do?" it asked, glancing at me.

"It was supposed to make you stumble," I said. "But, it'll work as a distraction too."

At that moment, Bastille tackled him.

Kiliman yelled, falling to the ground, the Crystin blade sliding from his grip. As he hit, something fell from one of his pockets and skidded across the floor.

My Translator's Lenses.

I cried out, dashing toward them. From behind, I could hear Bastille grunting as she snatched the Crystin blade. Kiliman, however, was just too strong. He grabbed her foot with a metal-bolt hand, then threw her to the side, causing her to drop the sword.

She hit the wall with a terrible thud. I spun in alarm.

Bastille slid to the ground. She looked dazed. Her forehead was bleeding from a cut, and one of her hands was still blue from the blast of frost. She favored her side and grimaced as she tried — then failed — to stand. She seemed to be in *really* bad shape.

Kiliman stood up, then recovered the Crystin blade. He shook his head, as if to clear it, and with his flesh hand he pulled out another Lens. The Voidstormer's Lens: the one that sucked things toward him.

He pointed the Lens toward Bastille. She groaned as she began to slide across the floor toward him, unable to even stand. Kiliman raised the sword.

I dived for the Translator's Lenses, which had skidded across the floor to rest beside one of the scroll-covered walls. I knelt beside the Lenses, hurriedly grabbing them.

"Ha!" Kiliman said. "You'd fetch those Lenses even as I kill your friend. I thought that Smedries were supposed to be bold and honorable. We can see what happens to your grand ideals once real danger is near!"

I knelt there for a moment, my back to Kiliman, Translator's Lenses in my fingers. I knew I couldn't let him have them. Not even to save my life or Bastille's . . .

I glanced over my shoulder. Bastille came to a rest in front of Kiliman. She had her eyes closed, and barely seemed to be breathing. He raised her mother's sword to kill her.

This is the part I've been warning you about. The part I know you're not going to like. I'm sorry.

I dashed away, making for the exit of the room.

Kiliman laughed even more loudly. "I knew it!"

At that moment, in my haste, I tripped. I stumbled on the uneven ground and fell facedown, the Translator's Lenses sliding from my fingers and hitting the stone floor. They tumbled away. "No!" I yelled.

"Aha!" Kiliman said, then spun his Voidstormer's Lens toward the fallen Translator's Lenses. They whipped off the floor and flew toward him. I watched the Lenses go, meeting Kiliman's eyes — one human, one glass — as he exulted in his victory.

Then I smiled. I think it was about that moment when he noticed the trip wire tied around the frame of the Translator's Lenses, which flew through the air toward him.

A thin wire, nearly invisible. It stretched from the spectacles to a place across the room. The place where I'd been kneeling by the wall a moment before.

The place where I'd tied the other end of the trip wire to one of the scrolls.

Kiliman caught the Lenses. The trip wire pulled taut. The scroll popped off of its shelf, falling to the ground.

The Librarian monster's eyes opened wide, and his mouth gaped in shock. The Translator's Lenses fell to the ground in front of him.

Immediately, the Curators surrounded Kiliman. "You have taken a book!" one cried.

"No!" Kiliman said, stepping back. "It was an accident!"

"You signed no contract," another said, skull face smiling. "Yet you took a book."

"Your soul is ours."

"*NO!*"

I shuddered at the pain in that voice. Kiliman reached toward me, furious, but it was too late. A fire grew from nothing at his feet. It burned around him, and he screamed again.

"You will fall, Smedry! The Librarians will have your blood! It will be spilt on an altar to make the very Lenses we'll use to destroy your kingdoms, break that which you love, and enslave those who follow you. You may have beaten me, but *you will fall!*"

I shivered. The fires consumed Kiliman, and I had to shield my eyes against the bright light.

And then, it was gone. I blinked, clearing the after-image from my eyes, and saw a new Curator — one with only half of a skull — hovering where Kiliman had stood. A group of discarded nuts, bolts, gears, and springs were scattered on the ground.

The half-skull Curator hovered over to the side of the room, carefully replacing the scroll that had been pulled free. I ignored it; there were more important things to worry about.

"Bastille!" I said, rushing over to her. There was blood on her lips, and she seemed so bruised and battered. I knelt beside her.

She groaned softly. I gulped.

"Nice trick," she whispered. "With the trip wire."

"Thanks."

She coughed, then spit up some blood.

By the first sands, I thought with a sudden stab of fear. *No. This can't be happening!*

"Bastille, I . . ." I suddenly found tears in my eyes. "I wasn't fast enough or smart enough. I'm sorry."

"What are you blathering about?"

I blinked. "Well, you look kind of bad, and . . ."

"Shut up and help me to my feet," she said, stumbling to her knees.

I stared at her.

"What?" she said. "It's not like I'm dying or anything. I just broke a few ribs and bit my tongue. Shattering Glass, Smedry, do you have to be so melodramatic all the time?"

With that, she stretched, grimaced, and stumbled over to pick up the fallen Crystin sword.

I got to my feet, feeling relieved and a little foolish. I went over and carefully untied the Translator's Lenses from the trip wire, then slid them into their pocket, where they belonged. To the side, I could see Kaz peek into the room, apparently having returned from depositing Draulin and Australia somewhere safe. He smiled broadly when he saw me and Bastille, then rushed into the room.

"Alcatraz, kid, I can't believe you're still alive!"

"I know," I said. "I thought for sure one of us was going to die. You know, if I ever write my memoirs, this section is going to seem really boring because nobody was narratively dynamic enough to get themselves killed."

Bastille snorted, joining us, holding one of her arms close to her side. "That's real inspiring, Smedry."

"You're the one who stopped following the plan," I said.

"What? Kiliman was faster than you. How exactly were you planning to keep him from chasing you down as you ran?"

"I'm . . . not sure," I admitted.

Kaz just laughed. "What happened to Kiliman anyway?"

I pointed toward the Curator with half of a skull. "He's doing a little bit of soul-searching," I said. "You could say that watching over these books is his *soul* responsibility now. He'll probably enjoy the *soul*-itary lifestyle."

"Can I hit him?" Bastille asked flatly.

I smiled, then noticed something on the ground. I picked it up — a single, yellow Lens.

"What's that?"

"Tracker's Lens," I said. "Kiliman's. It had been in the pouch with Draulin's Fleshstone."

"My mother," Bastille said. "How is she?"

"I'm fine," Draulin's voice said. We spun to find her standing beside a sheepish Australia in the doorway.

"Fine" was a stretch — Draulin still looked pale, like someone who had been sick for far too long. Yet, her step was steady as she walked into the room and joined us.

"Lord Smedry," she said, going down on one knee. "I've failed you."

"Nonsense," I said.

"The Librarian of the Scrivener's Bones captured me," she said. "I was caught in a trap, tied up, and he was able to take me without any trouble. I have shamed my order."

I rolled my eyes. "The rest of us got caught in Curator traps too. We were just lucky enough to wiggle out of them before Kiliman found us."

Draulin still bowed her head. On the back of her neck, I caught sight of a sparkling crystal — her Fleshstone, replaced.

"Get up and stop apologizing," I said. "I'm serious. You did well. You forced a confrontation with Kiliman, and we won that confrontation. So, consider yourself part of our victory."

Draulin stood up, though she didn't appear appeased. She fell into her traditional parade-rest stance, looking straight ahead. "As you wish, Lord Smedry."

"Mother," Bastille said.

Draulin looked down.

"Here," Bastille said, holding up the Crystin blade.

I blinked in shock. For some reason, I'd been expecting Bastille to keep that.

Draulin hesitated for a moment, then took the sword. "Thank you," she said, then sheathed it on her back. "What are your plans now, Lord Smedry?"

"I'm . . . not sure yet," I said.

"Then I will set up a perimeter around this room." Draulin bowed to me, then walked over to the entrance and took up a guard position. Bastille moved toward the other entrance, but I grabbed her arm.

"That woman should be begging for your forgiveness."

"Why?" Bastille asked.

"You're in so much trouble because you lost your sword," I said. "Well, Draulin didn't do much better now, did she?"

"But she got hers back."

"So?"

"So, she didn't break it."

"Only because of us."

"No," Bastille said, "because of *you*, Alcatraz. Kiliman defeated me — just like the Alivened in the downtown Library did. You had to save me both times."

"I . . ."

Bastille carefully removed my hand from her arm. "I appreciate it, Smedry. I really do. I'd be dead several times over if it wasn't for you."

With that, she walked away. Never before had a thank-you seemed so despondent to my ears.

Things aren't going to get fixed that easily, I thought. *Bastille still considers herself a failure.*

We're going to have to do something about that.

"You going to destroy that, kid?" Kaz asked.

I glanced down, realizing that I still had Kiliman's Tracker's Lens in my fingers.

"It's *very* Dark Oculary," Kaz said, rubbing his chin. "Blood-forged Lenses are bad business."

"We *should* destroy it, then," I said. "At least turn it over to someone who knows what to do with it. I . . ."

I trailed off. (Obviously.)

"What?" Kaz asked.

I didn't answer. I'd caught something through the Tracker's Lens. I held it up to my eye and was surprised to see footprints on the ground. There were lots of them, of course. Mine, Bastille's, even Kiliman's — though those were fading quickly, since I didn't know him well. More important, however, I saw three sets of footprints that were very distinct. All led toward a small, inconspicuous door on the far side of the room.

One set of footprints was Grandpa Smedry's. Another set of yellowish black ones belonged to my mother. The final set, a blazing red-white, was undoubtedly that of my father. All went through the doorway, but there were no sets leading back out.

"Hey," I said, turning to the nearest Curator. "What's through that door?"

"That's where we keep the possessions of those who have been turned into Curators," the creature said in a raspy voice. Indeed, I saw several Curators cleaning up the remnants of Kiliman's transformation — the bits of metal and the clothing he had been wearing.

I lowered the Tracker's Lens. "Come on," I said to the others. "We almost forgot the reason why we came here in the first place."

"And what was that reason again?" Kaz asked.

I pointed at the door. "To find out what's on the other side of that."

CHAPTER 20

Hangook Mal Malha GiMa Ship Shio.

Expectations. They are among the most important things in all of existence. (Which is amusing because, being abstract concepts, you could argue that they don't even "exist" at all.)

Everything we do, everything we experience, and everything we say is clouded by our expectations. We go to school or work in the mornings because we expect that it will be rewarding. (Or, at least, we expect that if we don't, we'll get in trouble.)

We build friendships based on expectations. We expect our friends to act in a certain way, and then we act as they expect us to. Indeed, the very fact that we get up in the mornings shows that we expect the sun to rise, the world to keep spinning, and our shoes to fit, just like they all did the day before.

People have real trouble when you upset their expectations. For instance, you likely didn't expect me to begin this chapter writing in Korean. Though, after the bunny-bazooka story, one begins to wonder how you can possibly maintain any expectations about this book at all.

And that, my friends, is the point.

Half of you reading this book live in the Hushlands. I was a Hushlander myself, once, and I am not so naïve as to assume that you all believe my story is true. You probably read my first book, thought it was fun. You're reading this one, not because you believe its text, but because you *expected* another fun story.

Expectations. We rely on them. That's why so many Hushlanders have trouble believing the Free Kingdoms and the Librarian conspiracy. You don't *expect* to wake up and discover that everything you know about history, geography, and politics is wrong.

So, perhaps you can begin to see why I've included some of the things I have. Bunnies with bazookas, ships that get repaired (more on that later), faces made of numbers, editorials from short people about how we regard the world, and a lesson on shoes and fish. All of these examples try to prove that you need to have an open mind. Because not everything you believe is true, and not everything you expect to happen will.

Maybe this book will mean nothing to you. Maybe my tale of demonic Curators and magical Lenses will pass you by as pure silliness, to be read but then forgotten. Perhaps because this story deals with people who are far away — and, perhaps, not even real at all — you will assume it doesn't relate to you.

I hope not. Because, you see, I have expectations too, and they whisper to me that you'll understand.

We found a long hallway on the other side of the door. At the end of that hallway was another door, and on the other side of that door was a small chamber.

It had one occupant. He sat on a dusty crate, staring down at the ground in front of him. He was not locked in. He simply seemed to have been sitting there, thinking.

And crying.

"Grandpa Smedry?" I asked.

Leavenworth Smedry, Oculator Dramatus, friend of kings and potentates, looked up. It had only been a few days since I'd last seen him, but it felt like so much longer. He smiled at me, eyes sorrowful.

"Alcatraz, lad," he said. "Huddling Hales, you *did* follow me!"

I rushed forward, grabbing him in an embrace. Kaz and Australia followed me in, Bastille and Draulin taking up positions by the door.

"Hey, Pop," Kaz said, raising a hand.

"Kazan!" Grandpa Smedry said. "Well, well. Been corrupting your nephew, I assume?"

Kaz shrugged. "Somebody needs to."

Grandpa Smedry smiled, but there was something . . . sorrowful about even that expression. He wasn't his usual lively self. Even the little tufts of hair behind his ears seemed less perky.

"Grandpa, what is it?" I asked.

"Oh, nothing, lad," Grandpa Smedry said, hand on my shoulder. "I . . . really should have been done grieving by now. I mean, your father has been gone for thirteen years! I still kept hope, all that time. I thought for sure we'd find him here. I arrived too late, it seems."

"What do you mean?" I asked.

"Oh, I didn't show you, did I?" He handed something out to me. A note. "I found this in the room. Your mother had already been here, it seems, and collected Attica's belongings. Clever one, that Shasta. Always a step ahead of me, even without my Talent interfering. She was in and out of the Library before we even arrived. Yet, she left this behind. I wonder why."

I looked down, reading the note.

Old man, it said.

I assume you got my letter telling you that Attica was coming to the Library of Alexandria. By now you probably realize that we were both too late to stop him from doing something foolish. He always was an idiot.

I've confirmed that he gave up his soul, but for what purpose, I cannot fathom. Those blasted Curators won't tell me anything useful. I've taken his possessions. It's my right, whatever you may claim, as his wife.

I know you don't care for me. I return the sentiment. I am sad to see Attica finally gone, though. He shouldn't have had to die in such a silly way.

The Librarians now have the tools we need to defeat you. It's a shame we couldn't come to an agreement. I don't care if you believe me about Attica *or not. I thought I should leave this note. I owe him that much.*

Shasta Smedry

I looked up from the note, frustrated.

There were still tears in Grandpa Smedry's eyes, and he wasn't looking at me. He just stared at the wall, eyes unfocused. "Yes, I should have grieved long ago. I'm late to that, it appears. Late indeed . . ."

Kaz read over my shoulder. "Nutmeg!" he swore, pointing at the note. "We don't believe this, do we? Shasta's a lying Librarian rat!"

"She's not lying, Kazan," Grandpa Smedry said. "At least not about your brother. The Curators confirmed it, and they cannot lie. Attica has become one of them."

Nobody objected to Grandpa Smedry's assertion. It was the truth. I could feel it. With the Tracker's Lens, I could even see the place where my father's tracks ended. My mother's tracks, however, left by a different door.

The ground at my feet began to crack, my Talent sensing my frustration, and I felt like pounding on something. We'd come all this way, just to be turned away at the end. Why? Why had my father done something so foolish?

"He always was too curious for his own good," Kaz said softly, laying a hand on Grandpa Smedry's shoulder. "I told him it would lead him to a bad end."

Grandpa Smedry nodded. "Well, he has the knowledge he always wanted. He can read book upon book, learn anything he wants."

With that, he stood. We joined him, making our way out of the hallway. We walked through the central room and out into the stacks beyond, trailed by a couple of Curators who were — undoubtedly — hoping we'd make one last-minute mistake and lose our souls.

I sighed, then turned and gave one final glance at the place where my father had ended his life. There, above the doorway, I saw the scribbles. The ones scratched into the stone. I frowned, then pulled out the Translator's Lenses and put them on. The message was simple, only one sentence long.

I am not an idiot.

I blinked. Grandpa Smedry and Kaz were speaking softly about my father and his foolishness.

I am not an idiot.

What would prompt a person to give up his soul? Was

unlimited knowledge really worth that? Knowledge that you couldn't use? Couldn't share?

Unless . . .

I froze, causing the others to stop. I looked right at a Curator. "What happens when you write something down while you're in the Library?"

The creature seemed confused. "We take the writing from you and copy it. Then, we return the copy to you an hour later."

"And if you were to write something right before you gave up your soul?" I asked. "What if you were a Curator by the time the copy came back?"

The Curator glanced away.

"You cannot lie!" I said, pointing.

"I can choose not to speak."

"Not if property must be returned," I said, still pointing. "If my father wrote something before he was taken, then you wouldn't have had to give it to my mother unless she knew to ask for it. You *do* have to return it if I demand it. And I do. Give it to me."

The Curator hissed. Then, all of those standing around us hissed. I hissed back at them.

I'm . . . uh, not sure why I did that.

Finally, a Curator floated forward, carrying a slip of paper in its translucent hand. "This doesn't count as taking one of your books, does it?" I asked hesitantly.

"This is not ours," the Curator said, throwing the paper at my feet.

As the others stood around me, confused, I snatched up the paper and read it. It wasn't what I'd been expecting.

It's so simple, the paper read.

> The Curators are, like most things in this world, bound by laws. They are strange laws, but they are strong laws.
>
> The trick is to not own your own soul when you sign the contract. So, I bequeath my soul to my son, Alcatraz Smedry. I sign it away to him. He is its true owner.

I looked up.

"What is it, lad?" Grandpa Smedry asked.

"What would you do, Grandpa?" I asked. "If you were going to give up your soul not for a specific book, but because you wanted access to the Library's entire contents. What book would you ask for?"

Grandpa Smedry shrugged. "Vague Volskies, lad, I don't know! If you're just giving up your soul so that you can read the other books in the Library, it wouldn't matter which book you picked as the first, would it?"

"Actually, it would," I whispered. "The Library contains all the knowledge humans have ever known."

"So?" Bastille asked.

"So, it contains the solutions to every problem. I know what *I'd* ask for." I looked straight at the Curators. "I'd ask for the book that explained how to get my soul back after I'd given it to the Curators!"

There was a moment of stunned silence. The Curators suddenly began floating away from us.

"Curators!" I yelled. "This note bequeaths the soul of Attica Smedry to me! You have taken it unlawfully, and I demand it back!"

The creatures froze, then they began to scream in a howling, despairing cry.

One of them suddenly spun and threw back its hood, the fires in its eyes puffing out, replaced by human eyeballs. The skull bulged, growing the flesh of a hawk-faced, noble-looking man.

He tossed aside his robe, wearing a tuxedo underneath. "Aha!" he said. "I *knew* you'd figure it out, son!" The man turned, pointing at the hovering Curators. "Thank you kindly for the time you let me spend rummaging through your books, you old spooks! I beat you. I told you I would!"

"Oh, dear," Grandpa Smedry said, smiling. "We'll never shut him up now. He's gone and come back from the dead."

"It's him, then?" I asked. "My . . . father?"

"Indeed," Grandpa Smedry said. "Attica Smedry, in the flesh. Ha! I should have known. If ever there were a man to lose his soul and then find it again, it would be Attica!"

"Father, Kaz!" Attica said, walking over, putting an arm around each one. "We have work to do! The Free Kingdoms are in deep danger! Did you retrieve my possessions?"

"Actually," I said. "Your wife did that."

Attica froze, looking back at me. Even though he'd addressed me earlier, it seemed that now he was seeing me for the first time. "Ah," he said. "She has my Translator's Lenses, then?"

"We assume so, son," Grandpa Smedry said.

"Well then, that means we have even *more* work to do!" And with that, my father strode down the hallway, walking as if he expected everyone to hop quickly and follow.

I stood, staring after him. Bastille and Kaz paused, looking at me.

"Not what you were expecting?" Bastille asked.

I shrugged. This was the first time I'd met my father, and he had barely glanced at me.

"He's just distracted, I'm sure," Bastille said. "A little addled from having spent so long as a ghost."

"Yeah," I said. "I'm sure that's it."

Kaz slapped me on the shoulder. "Don't get down, Al. This is a time for rejoicing!"

I smiled, his enthusiasm contagious. "I suppose you're right." We began to walk, my step growing a bit more springy. Kaz was right. True, everything wasn't perfect, but we *had* managed to save my father. Coming down into the Library had proven to be the best choice, in the end.

I might have been a bit inexperienced, but I'd made the right decision. I found myself feeling rather good as we walked.

"Thanks, Kaz," I said.

"For what?"

"For the encouragement."

He shrugged. "We short people are like that. Remember what I said about being more compassionate."

I laughed. "Perhaps. I do have to say, though — I've thought of at least *one* reason why it's better to be a tall person."

Kaz raised an eyebrow.

"Lightbulbs," I said. "If everyone were short like you, Kaz, then who'd change them?"

He laughed. "You're forgetting Reason number sixty-three, kid!"

"Which is?"

"If everyone were short, we could build lower ceilings! Think of how much we'd save on building costs!"

I laughed, shaking my head as we caught up to the others and made our way out of the Library.

EPILOGUE

THERE YOU GO. BOOK TWO OF MY MEMOIRS. IT'S NOT THE END, OF COURSE. YOU DIDN'T THINK IT WOULD BE, DID YOU? WE HAVEN'T EVEN GOTTEN TO THE PART WHERE I END UP TIED TO THAT ALTAR, ABOUT TO BE SACRIFICED! BESIDES, THESE THINGS ALWAYS COME IN TRILOGIES, AT LEAST. OTHERWISE THEY'RE NOT EPIC!

THIS VOLUME CONTAINED AN IMPORTANT SECTION OF MY LIFE. MY FIRST MEETING — HUMBLE THOUGH IT WAS — WITH THE FAMOUS ATTICA SMEDRY. MY FIRST REAL TASTE OF LEADERSHIP. MY FIRST CHANCE TO USE WINDSTORMER'S LENSES LIKE A JET ENGINE. (I NEVER GET TIRED OF THAT ONE.)

BEFORE WE PART, I OWE YOU ONE MORE EXPLANATION. IT HAS TO DO WITH A BOAT: THE SHIP OF THESEUS. DO YOU REMEMBER? EVERY PLANK IN IT HAD BEEN REPLACED, UNTIL IT LOOKED LIKE THE SAME SHIP, BUT WASN'T.

I TOLD YOU THAT I WAS THAT SHIP. PERHAPS NOW, AFTER READING THIS BOOK, YOU CAN SEE WHY.

YOU SHOULD NOW KNOW THE YOUNG ME PRETTY WELL. YOU'VE READ TWO BOOKS ABOUT HIM AND HAVE SEEN HIS PROGRESS AS A PERSON. YOU'VE EVEN SEEN HIM DO SOME HEROIC THINGS, LIKE CLIMB ON TOP OF A GLASS DRAGON, FACE DOWN A MEMBER OF THE SCRIVENER'S BONES, AND SAVE HIS FATHER FROM THE CLUTCHES OF THE CURATORS OF ALEXANDRIA.

YOU MAY WONDER WHY I'VE STARTED MY AUTOBIOGRAPHY SO FAR BACK, WHEN I STILL SHOWED HINTS THAT I MIGHT BE A GOOD PERSON. WELL, I'M THE SHIP OF THESEUS. I WAS ONCE THAT BOY, FULL OF HOPE, FULL OF POTENTIAL. THAT'S NOT WHO I AM ANYMORE. I'M A COPY. A FAKE.

I'M THE PERSON THAT YOUNG BOY GREW INTO, BUT I'M NOT HIM. I'M NOT THE HERO THAT EVERYONE SAYS — EVEN THOUGH I LOOK LIKE I SHOULD BE.

The purpose of this series is to show the changes I went through. To let you see the pieces of me slowly getting replaced until nothing is left of the original.

I'm a sad, pathetic person, writing his life story in the basement of a lavish castle he really doesn't deserve. I'm not a hero. Heroes don't let the people they love die.

I'm not proud of what I've become, but I intend to make certain that everyone knows the truth. It's time for the lies to end; time for people to realize that their Ship of Theseus is just a copy.

If the real one ever existed in the first place.

was not my place to say so.

"Bastille!" I screamed, holding her bloody body in my arms. "Why?"

She didn't respond. She just stared into the air, eyes glazed over, her spirit already gone. I shivered, pulling her close, but the body was growing cold.

"You can't die, you can't!" I said. "Please."

It was no use. Bastille was dead. Really dead. Deader than a battery left all night with the high beams on. So dead, she was twice as dead as anyone I'd ever seen dead. She was *that* dead.

"This is all my fault," I said. "I shouldn't have brought you in to fight Kiliman!"

I felt at her pulse, just in case. There was nothing. Because, you know, she was dead.

"Oh, cruel world," I said, sobbing.

I put a mirror up to her face to see if she was breathing. Of course, there was no mist on the mirror. Seeing as how Bastille was totally and completely dead.

"You were so young," I said. "Too young to be taken from us. Why did it have to happen to you, of all people, when you are so young? Too young to die, I mean."

I pricked her finger to make sure she wasn't just faking, but she didn't even flinch. I pinched her, then slapped her face. Nothing worked.

How many times do I have to explain that she was dead? I looked down at her body, her face turning blue from death, and I wept some more.

She was so dead that I didn't even realize that this section is in the book for two reasons. First, so that I could have Bastille die somewhere, just like I promised. (See, I wasn't lying about this! Ha!)

The second reason is, of course, so that if anyone skips forward to the end to read the last page — one of the most putrid and unholy things any reader can do — they will be shocked and annoyed to read that Bastille is dead.

The rest of you can ignore these pages. (Did I mention that Bastille is dead?)

The end.

About the Author

Brandon Sanderson is not, obviously, the real author of this book. Alcatraz Smedry wrote it. Because this book must be published in the Hushlands as a "fantasy" novel in order to confuse and distract Librarian agents, an arrangement has been reached with Mr. Sanderson to use his name on the cover.

Alcatraz has met Brandon Sanderson, and he was not impressed. Sanderson writes actual fantasy books — silly things that are nowhere near as factual and real as this text. He's the president of his local chapter of THCoFWWBAWTL, and he has been known to bring swords to weddings.

He's been imprisoned for improper use of puns on three separate occasions.

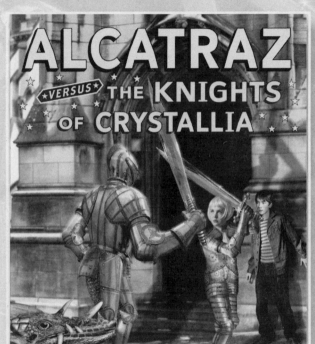